Emma:
lights!
camera!
cupcakes!

SIMON SPOTLIGHT

An imprint of Simon & Schuster Children's Publishing Division
1230 Avenue of the Americas, New York, New York 10020
Copyright © 2014 by Simon & Schuster, Inc.
All rights reserved, including the right of reproduction in whole or in part in any form.
SIMON SPOTLIGHT and colophon are registered
trademarks of Simon & Schuster, Inc.
Text by Elizabeth Doyle Carey
Chapter header illustrations by Maryam Choudhury
Designed by Laura Roode
For information about special discounts for bulk purchases, please contact
Simon & Schuster Special Sales
at 1-866-506-1949 or business@simonandschuster.com.
Manufactured in the United States of America 0314 OFF
First Edition 2 4 6 8 10 9 7 5 3 1
ISBN 978-1-4424-9930-0 (pbk)
ISBN 978-1-4424-9931-7 (hc)
ISBN 978-1-4424-9932-4 (eBook)
Library of Congress Catalog Card Number 2014930061

CUPCAKE DIARIES

Emma: lights! camera! cupcakes!

by coco simon

Simon Spotlight

New York   London   Toronto   Sydney   New Delhi

CHAPTER 1

The Topic of the Town

I love Fridays! Almost every Friday, my three best friends—Alexis, Mia, and Katie—and I have an official meeting and baking session for our Cupcake Club. Each week we try rotate where it takes place, so that makes it a little more interesting, and a lot of times we stretch it out into a sleepover too. It's just fun and kind of relaxing to know I don't have to worry about Friday plans. I'm always guaranteed to be chilling with my BFFs! It's also pretty cool to have something to look forward to all week.

Some weeks we have very little business to cover, but this week we had a lot! Alexis ran the meeting as usual.

"First on the agenda is a cupcake competition—birthday party for Isabel Gormley in two weeks.

She'd like two dozen unfrosted cupcakes; a mix of vanilla and chocolate—so half are chocolate cake and the other half are yellow cake. Then we'll send the frosting on the side, vanilla and chocolate. They are going to have a contest so all the kids can ice and decorate the cupcakes themselves."

"That is so cute!" cried Mia, lounging on my TV room sofa. "Wouldn't she maybe like some fondant roses on a sheet? Or containers of toppings?"

It's become almost boring for us to make basic cupcakes; we do it so rarely. We've made so many over-the-top cupcake designs in our day. Mia is very creative idea-wise, and Katie is great at execution. Alexis makes sure we charge properly for them. I'm good at promoting and networking to get us jobs.

"Actually, it would be cool to create a cupcake competition kit for parties. Maybe we could advertise that on our website!" I said.

Alexis tapped her pen with her teeth. "I agree. If we could get the pricing right, it might be worth offering it for a limited time to see how it does." She made some notes in her book. She's very strategic with how we spend our money, which is a good thing.

"Should we tint the vanilla frosting at least?"

suggested Katie. "We can give them different colors, like pink or purple . . . ?"

Alexis made some notes in her book. "I'll e-mail Mrs. Gormley and ask her, and also I'll see if she wants us to create the kit for them. The Gormleys are good clients. She'll probably be up for it."

I nodded. "What else is in the lineup?"

"We have the PTA meeting coming up, so let's do a complimentary order with fliers or little cards with our contact info to hand out. Maybe two dozen minis, since the parents don't eat much. Then"—Alexis consulted her notes—"we have a retirement party for Emma's mom's friend at work, another librarian. They'd like us to do something pretty. . . . There are your fondant roses, Mia! And that about wraps it up. Anything else?"

Katie nodded and held up a sheet of paper torn from a magazine. "I want to try this new pink-lemonade frosting. It's supposed to be delicious, and it might be cute for a light, floral spring cupcake."

Alexis noted it, and we all agreed. Then there was a pause, and Mia looked up with a devilish grin. "Can we just gossip now for a minute about the number-one topic in town?"

Alexis groaned and put her hands over her eyes. "When will it end?" she cried.

Katie and I grinned at each other. "Do you have a new scoop?" I asked Mia.

"No! I thought you might, of all people, since you're so buddy-buddy with Romaine!"

The topic of the town was that Romaine Ford, our one and only homegrown superstar—model turned actress, singer, Oscar winner, and more— is premiering her new movie right here in Maple Grove in just a week! Already shopkeepers are offering premiere promotions and decorating their store windows like it's the Academy Awards. It's sort of annoying because everyone acts like they're Romaine Ford's best friend, or like she shops at their stores all the time, which they aren't and she doesn't. Even the local paper has been going around and interviewing people about her, who I'm sure don't even know her, which drives me nuts.

I, on the other hand, do know Romaine Ford.

I don't know her well, but we are *almost* what you might call friends. It's kind of a long story, but I met her when I was modeling bridesmaid dresses at the store where she bought her wedding gown. Then my friends and I made cupcakes for her wedding shower, and she came to my talent show at camp. That was a pretty big deal. We haven't stayed in touch or anything, but

4

I know if we were walking past each other on the street and I said, "Hi, Romaine!" she'd say, "Hi, Emma!" back.

I'm sure I will have more information tomorrow since I'm working at The Special Day bridal salon, which I do every other weekend, modeling dresses and helping out. Tomorrow she'll be coming in for a dress fitting with her bridesmaids, and I'll be delivering the salon's weekly cupcake order and staying on to help Mona, the owner of the store. The only thing is, as an employee, I'm always sworn to secrecy about brides (especially Romaine!) and their details. This can be frustrating and hard, since I'm so used to telling my friends everything. It's just that I'm so dying to tell them I'm seeing Romaine tomorrow that I might burst! I looked down at my nails. If Alexis were to look at my face, she'd totally know I was hiding something.

Since our Cupcake business meeting was finished for the day, we moved into the kitchen to start baking, and our conversation continued as we ran down all the things we knew about Romaine Ford's new movie. It's a love story, set in the past, with a lot of other famous stars, all of whom are coming to the red carpet premiere at the theater where my friends and I usually hang out! It's so insane! It's like a dream to think these actors and actresses will be here, maybe even sitting in my usual favorite seat; seventh row from the front, second seat in on the left. There will be tons of press and other Hollywood bigwigs there, plus of course Romaine Ford's handsome fiancé, the gorgeous Liam Carey, an actor and director who does all sorts of volunteer work in Africa in his spare time.

"We should try to go and watch them on the red carpet!" suggested Katie, the most starstruck of us all.

"Yes!" agreed Mia. "And we can get dressed up!"

We all laughed since Mia the fashionista will look for any excuse to get decked out.

"I can wear my dress from Dylan's sweet sixteen," said Alexis decisively, and we all laughed again since Alexis is usually so reluctant to get dressed up.

"Okay, let's focus on work for a minute," I said. I couldn't keep talking about Romaine Ford and not spill the beans. "We need to make five dozen mini cupcakes for Mona—she wants half of the vanilla-vanilla combo and half cinnamon bun with cream cheese frosting for tomorrow morning. And that's it, right?"

"Yes, but do you guys mind if I make this pink-lemonade frosting right now on the side? Maybe make an extra half dozen cupcakes and we can sample it?" asked Katie.

"Yum! Sample what?" said my oldest brother, Sam, walking into the kitchen from the mudroom.

"Sam!" cried my friends, which was both heart-warming and annoying. I have two older brothers, Sam and Matt, and one younger one, Jake, and they are all pretty irritating to me (Sam the least, actually), but my friends adore them. Mia and Katie baby Jake, Alexis is practically dating Matt, who's a year older than us, and Mia and Katie both have massive crushes on Sam (who I do have to admit is good-looking).

"Sample nothing, mister!" I scolded.

"Emma!" chided Mia.

"My brand-new pink-lemonade frosting. I don't care what Emma says—you're our official tester," declared Katie.

"No way!" I protested. "These guys will eat anything. Just slather some frosting on an old shoe, and Sam and the other guys will wolf it down and say it's delicious. They're totally indiscriminating!"

Sam came over and gave me a noogie while I shrieked. Then Matt came in with Jake, and suddenly it seemed there were boys everywhere, peering into bowls and sniffing the air.

"Out!" I commanded. "It's my kitchen time! We'll call you back if there's something to sample, okay? You're like a pack of wild hounds."

Jake and Matt howled and woofed like wild hounds, but they all finally left, with my friends in varying degrees of the giggles. It was very quiet once the boys were gone, at least in the kitchen, but I could still hear them horsing around in the den. We worked in silence for a minute, and then the conversation turned, of course, back to Romaine.

"When is she getting married?" asked Katie.

"I don't know," I said. "I would figure it's probably within the next month or two; it was a while ago that she ordered the dress." *And since she's coming in for her fitting tomorrow,* I added silently. The fitting is when they hem and alter the dress so it fits perfectly. Most brides have a few fittings close to the wedding day to make sure the dress is just right. Some are really picky and have, like, five or six, but most have around three. I knew Romaine was only having two fittings due to her schedule, so her wedding must be soon.

I kind of felt bad for Romaine. Most brides came in for their fittings with some friends and family, and it was always like a little party. Mona

8

was coordinating how to sneak Romaine into the store so no one would try to take pictures or bother her. Trying to keep quiet like this makes me realize how hard it must be to be famous, with so many people caring about your every move. Imagine if someone was taking a picture of you every time you went to the supermarket or out to eat. I know they pay stars a lot, but really, they are never actually off duty. Work is full time and for life, if they do it well.

We finished up our baking duties, and Katie's pink-lemonade frosting turned out really well. It was a pretty, pale pink color and tasted exactly like lemonade.

"Come and get it, troops!" Katie hollered out the kitchen door, and then there was a stampede. The girls and I stood back while my brothers gorged themselves on the extra cupcakes with either lemonade or vanilla frosting.

I rolled my eyes. "Are they good?" I asked loudly.

"Umm-hmmm." Matt nodded emphatically.

"Yesss!" said Jake as crumbs tumbled out of his mouth.

"The vanilla are delicious. A little plain. The lemonade . . . ," said Sam.

Uh-oh. *He won't really say something mean about*

Katie's new frosting, will he? I worried, but I didn't need to. Good old Sammy.

"The lemonade ones are insane!"

Katie beamed like she was being photographed at a movie premiere. "Thanks!" she said happily.

I bit my tongue to keep from saying anything again about Sam not being very picky. I wanted Katie to enjoy the compliment.

"Any more?" asked Matt after eating two. He looked all around the counter to see if we were hiding some.

"That's it, mister. You can't eat up all our profits!" teased Alexis.

"I'll pay!" said Matt, reaching into his pocket.

"Oh please. Like you can afford our cupcakes!" said Alexis, swatting him with a dish towel.

"Well, maybe if you didn't charge one hundred dollars per cupcake," teased Matt. They were both laughing and looking at each other all googly-eyed, and I wanted to barf so I had to turn away. Sometimes it's superfun and convenient to have your best friend like your brother, and other times it's superannoying.

For example, later that night, all the Cupcakers went to my room to change into our pj's before we watched a movie downstairs. But this time Alexis refused to change into her pj's. I thought it was odd, but then I got it. She didn't want to wear her pj's in front of Matt.

It's just little stuff like that that adds up. I'd never say anything to Alexis though because then she would be sorry but also a little mad, and I wouldn't want to start all that up. I had enough trouble with trying to keep my bridal salon work a secret from my friends, never mind alienating them officially.

Sometimes it's so complicated just being me that I can't imagine how Romaine Ford is her.

CHAPTER 2

Wedding Cupcakes

$\mathcal{I}$ got up early to shower and blow-dry my hair since Mona had warned me that I might do a little modeling today. The other girls were up and eating cereal when I came out of the bathroom; Mia and Katie were in their cute pj's, but Alexis was fully dressed, of course. I sighed. I kind of wished I could hang out with these guys rather than work this morning.

"Lookin' good, Emma!" said Mia approvingly.

"Thanks," I said with a smile as I grabbed a bowl off the counter.

"Very pretty, sweetheart," said my mother, coming to plant a kiss on my cheek.

"Yeah, *sweetheart*," sang Matt as he strode into the kitchen, also fully dressed. Usually, if he doesn't have sports, he sleeps late and then spends as long as possible in his pj bottoms and a ratty old T-shirt. Hmm.

"Can it, mister," I said.

"Kids!" warned my mom. I glared at Matt.

"Looking pretty spiffy yourself there. Going somewhere?" Now I was annoyed and wanted to embarrass him.

"Wouldn't you like to know?" he said sarcastically as he pulled out a stool from the counter and sat. My dig had not fazed him at all. Annoying. Alexis had her back to him, but I could tell by her face that she was totally attuned to his every move, even though she couldn't see him.

"Actually, I wouldn't," I said. "I'm sure it's something gross." I wanted to tease him that he was going to meet a girl, but I realized that would hurt Alexis's feelings, and I couldn't very well tease him about her with her there. Ugh! Now I couldn't wait for this sleepover to end, so I could get to work.

"Em, we'll go in five minutes, okay?" said my mom. "I'm just going to run upstairs for a sweater. Girls, I'm not kicking you out—you're welcome to stay as long as you like—but if anyone wants a ride home, you can come with us and I'll drop you off after I drop Emma at the store."

13

Mia and Katie were heading into the city to see Mia's dad, so they had their plans set. I looked at Alexis, who I knew wished she could stay, but staying without me here would be really weird. She struggled for a minute, then said, "I'll come with you, Mrs. Taylor. Thanks!" She stood to take her bowl to the sink, and I watched her try to avoid looking at Matt. But then he said something totally lame, like "Rushing off to work on a business plan, boss lady?" She started giggling like she'd been waiting for any excuse to laugh with him, and I wanted to puke.

I shoveled in my last bite of cereal and went to get my coat. Katie and Mia said they'd call Mia's mom for a ride to the train station and would clean up the air mattresses and blankets in my room before they left. I glanced at Alexis and saw her struggle again with the idea of staying, but now it was kind of too late; she had to follow through on leaving with me. I hugged Mia and Katie and got into the car while Alexis went up to get her bag.

A minute later my mom hopped in and said, "Are we taking Alexis?"

I rolled my eyes and said, "You mean Matt's girl-friend, Alexis?"

My mom laughed. "She does like Matt, doesn't

14

she? It's cute. Puppy love! So sweet."

"Puppy puke!" I said, crossing my arms tightly.

"Oh, Emma, don't be a bad sport. It's very safe to have a crush on your best friend's brother. I had one on my friend Sandy's brother when I was a girl."

"What did Sandy think about that?"

"She didn't mind. I don't think."

"Aha! But you don't *know*!"

"Well . . . we lost touch."

"See?"

Just then Alexis got into the car, and my mom gave me a knowing smile. I was too annoyed to even turn around.

"All set?" my mom said to Alexis.

"Yup! Thanks!" said Alexis, closing the door and buckling up.

"Oh! I forgot the cupcakes!" I said, smacking my forehead. I began unbuckling my seat belt as I reached for my door handle.

"Got 'em," said Alexis. She patted the cupcake carrier, and it made a hollow thunking sound in the back.

"Oh. Thanks," I said. I guess Alexis isn't all bad. I mean, she has been my best friend for my whole life. I turned around to smile at her, and she smiled back. She had no idea I was annoyed at her, and, honestly, why should I be? It wasn't her fault she liked my brother. And it wasn't her fault he liked her back. Actually, maybe it would be worse if he didn't like her back. I sighed and listened to my mom and Alexis discuss the big premiere the whole way to the mall. It took all my self control to not yell, "And I'm going to see Romaine in a few minutes!"

When I got to the usually serene The Special Day, it was chaos. Controlled chaos. And that only means one thing.

"Emma! Hiiiiii!" said Patricia, Mona's assistant, as she flew past me with an armload of white cut flowers.

"Daaarling!" said Mona as she sailed across the room to fluff the sofa cushions.

I turned to one of the salesgirls hurrying past and said, "Big customer here yet?"

She winked at me and shook her head. "Not yet," she said.

I smiled in excitement. "Mona, I'll go set up the cupcakes, then let me know what I can do to help," I called. I went into the back where they have a tiny kitchen and began to plate the cupcakes on one of

Mona's beautiful three-tiered china display platters.

Patricia came in to fill a vase with more water.

"She's coming in today, right?" I whispered.

She nodded and smiled. "The second to last fitting, actually!"

"Wait, so then it's just the final fitting, which is always the day before the wedding, right?"

"Yup!" said Patricia with a wink.

"And that would be when . . . ?"

"Can't tell!" she sang, and then she flitted out of the room.

"Patricia!" I complained as she skipped away, and I could hear her laughter floating back through the hall. I knew I'd find out sooner or later, though. I always do.

Sure enough, Romaine arrived with her mom, her sister, and three bridesmaids, one of whom was the famous singer and piano player (and fashion model), Samantha Holmes, right before the store opened! I was peeking out from a dressing room, and I saw them all walk in. I wasn't sure if they'd need me in there or just as a runner (that's someone who runs and gets things, like a different size or more pins), so I stayed put until further instructions. But soon I heard Mona calling me, and I left my little cocoon and walked slowly to the largest of the private dressing rooms Mona uses for brides. I had butterflies in my stomach, and now I wasn't so confident Romaine would remember me. I mean, she must meet thousands of people a year!

I opened the door and ducked inside, already blushing. And then I heard, "Emma!"

"There she is!"

"Hey, Emma!"

And Romaine crossed the room to give me a big hug. I couldn't believe it!

"I—I wasn't sure you'd remember me. Th-thanks!" I stammered awkwardly.

"Remember you? How could we forget? Between the wonderful cupcakes for my shower and your great job at the camp talent show and all your cute friends!" Romaine was beaming at me and suddenly I felt like I was the star and she was the fan. It was amazing! I laughed.

"Oh, you look just as pretty as ever, dear!" said Mrs. Ford from across the room. Mona had given me a bridesmaid's dress to wear. I usually wore different dresses when I was at the store, so the brides could see how they looked on an actual person. The one I was wearing today had a really pretty pink satin bow.

"Thanks," I said, playing with the bow. Then I

stopped. Mona always told me not to fuss with the dresses—especially when I'm wearing them.

Mona was smiling proudly at me, and I smiled back. Then she said, "Now, we have lots of Emma's cupcakes for this morning, so, Emma, why don't you run and get us some of those, please, and then we'll see if we need you to stand in again as a fit model for Romaine's niece. Meanwhile, Patricia and I will go get the dresses, and the bridal party can try them on."

I scurried out to get the cupcakes, and when I returned I passed them out on small linen napkins, the way Mona had shown me. Everyone took one, and it was pretty quiet for a minute as they all savored the treats.

"Oh! These are so delicious!" said Samantha, nibbling on a vanilla cupcake. "I could eat a hundred of them, but then my dress won't fit!" She laughed.

I smiled at her, glad to have a chance to make eye contact. I was so used to seeing her on YouTube music videos, playing the piano and singing: her long arms toned in a sleeveless gown, gracefully outstretched while she sang and played the piano without even looking down at the keys. She even played at this past year's Super Bowl halftime show, watched by a billion people! It was too weird to see her here, sitting in front of me in jeans and a T-shirt.

"They could let it out for you," said Romaine's sister Florence with a wink.

"My manager would kill me!" said Samantha.

"Oh, these managers are so ruthless! Mine tells me every pound shaves a hundred thousand dollars off my paycheck," Romaine said, groaning.

A hundred thousand dollars!

"Girls," scolded Mrs. Ford.

"Sorry," said Romaine. "Tacky to talk about money in public!"

Mrs. Ford nodded approvingly, and Romaine rolled her eyes like a teenager. "Mom's the boss," she said with a shrug.

"Sorry, Mrs. F.," said Samantha.

"You girls are talented enough to not have to talk like that," said Mrs. Ford with a sniff.

Wow, I thought. Mrs. Ford had power. Imagine scolding a three-time Grammy Award winner, and an Oscar winner, at the same time! Then I thought about it. After all, Mrs. Ford was still just Romaine's mom, even if Romaine was a big star. My mom would probably still correct me if I had bad manners about something too, even if I was a movie star.

"Let's have another, then!" Samantha giggled,

and I circled back to her with the platter.

She popped a cinnamon one into her mouth this time. "Mmmm! That one is just as delicious as the other! Romaine, maybe you should have a *cinnamon*-flavored wedding cake! That would solve all your troubles!"

I looked at Romaine and saw her sigh.

"I love Liam so much, but the one thing we can't agree on is a wedding cake. He thinks that big fancy white wedding cakes are old-fashioned, and I kind of agree, but I'm not going to reinvent the wheel, you know?"

I passed the platter to Romaine, and she selected another vanilla cupcake.

"Oh, Emma, these really are the best. Too bad you don't make wedding cakes!"

"Hey!" said Romaine's sister, who looks a lot like her. "I saw on that TV show *Cupcake Connections* that they did a cupcake tower for a wedding. It was really pretty!"

I wanted to say the Cupcake Club *had* actually done a cupcake tower for Mia's mom's wedding and for a bridal fashion show, but I didn't want to get too involved in their conversation. I was just there as a server after all. Mona had been pretty strict when I started working at the salon that I wasn't really supposed to chat with everyone. I was supposed to be working.

"Yes, but where do you think would we find someone who . . ." Suddenly, Romaine stopped and turned to look at me. Then everyone was looking at me. I blushed and looked down just as Mona and Patricia burst back into the room with the rack of dresses.

"Here we go!" said Mona.

"YOU!" said Romaine.

I looked up. "Me?"

Mona looked both worried and confused. "Everything all right in here?" she asked.

Romaine had crossed the room, her cheeks suddenly pink and her eyes shining with excitement. "Emma! Would you make cupcakes for my wedding?"

I thought I was going to faint. I put my hand to my chest. "Me?" I croaked.

"Yes, you!" cried Romaine.

CHAPTER 3

Stop the Presses!

$\mathcal{M}$ona clapped her hands and said, "That's a lovely idea, but let's get people started on their fittings, and then you can work out those details later. I know you ladies have limited time today. Romaine, would you like to come first, please? Right this way."

Still smiling, Romaine crossed the room and called, "I *love* this idea!" before she drew the curtain across the fitting room. Mona swished in behind her, a large white garment bag over her arm. Mona was wearing her white gloves, as usual. She never wants to leave a mark on any of the expensive fabrics or embroideries that the store features, so she wears white gloves when she's touching the gowns. At first it seemed a little silly, but once, I accidentally got some frosting on a white dress I was wearing, and I learned the hard way you have to be really, really careful.

Mona and Romaine chatted behind the curtain, while everyone else around the room chatted. I put down the cupcakes and passed iced water in small plastic party cups, which people gratefully gulped down. Chatting was thirsty work.

Moments later the curtain was pulled back and Mona happily announced, "Ladies, here comes the bride!" And out stepped Romaine.

Everyone in the room gasped. Romaine looked incredible! The dress was a simple, with white lace on top and a fitted white bodice underneath it, and little cap sleeves. The gown ballooned out into a princess-type bottom, with a big skirt made of a thick satin that glowed a pearly white and swished from side to side as Romaine walked.

"Oh, darling!" said Mrs. Ford, and she began to cry. I almost cried too, but instead I jumped to get the tissue box from the sideboard and brought it over to Mrs. Ford, where she laughed and gratefully plucked a few tissues.

"*Oh!*" She mopped her eyes. "You look more beautiful than I've ever seen!" she said to her daughter, and that was saying something.

Romaine twirled and looked at the dress in the mirror, smiling so, so happily.

"Awesome!" her sister said breathlessly.

"Girl, you look g-l-a-m-o-r-o-u-s, glamorous!" sang Samantha.

"I love it, Mona!" said Romaine sweetly. "It's the prettiest dress I've ever worn. And it's so comfortable! I thought it might be heavy or scratchy, but it's not. I feel totally relaxed in it." She spun around again.

"It's divine, dear, just divine!" said Mona. A row of pins between her clenched teeth made her talk kind of funny, but I was used to it. She got Romaine to stand still and then squatted, pinning the hem at the back of the dress and then standing to pin the bodice. "Please do make sure you're eating enough cupcakes, though, because if I need to take this top part in any more at the final fitting, I'll have to detach it and rework it to fit," said Mona with a grin. "It won't be easy!"

"Didja hear that, Sammy?" Romaine cackled. "Call my manager and tell him! More cupcakes! Mona's orders!"

"Uh-uh, you tell him yourself!" said Samantha, all fake-scared.

I smiled, watching them.

25

Romaine was so cute. She kept looking at the dress in the mirror and just grinning from ear to ear. "I can't wait until Liam sees me in this dress. That will be the highlight of the day for me. The look on his face as soon as I start down the aisle."

I was dying to know when the big day was, but I couldn't ask. It wouldn't have been appropriate. I just held the tray with the pins for Mona as Romaine turned very slowly around and Mona pinned a little bit at a time.

Soon, Mona was finished and Romaine went to change out of the dress and then her maid of honor went in. That was when Romaine said, "Mona, I'm stealing your star for a minute to talk business." She perched on the side of the sofa in her jeans, T-shirt, and socks and looked like she could have been one of my old babysitters rather than an international star.

"Okay, Emma, let's get down to details. We're having a hundred guests, so I'd figure if you do full-size cupcakes, you'd want . . ."

"We usually do a fifteen percent overage," I said, feeling very professional using an Alexis business term. That meant for a hundred people, we'd make one hundred and fifteen cupcakes.

"Great. Maybe do twenty percent," Romaine said, a mischievous sparkle in her eyes. "I can exercise on my honeymoon."

"Got it." I smiled conspiratorially, then asked, "And when do you need them?" I was figuring she wouldn't need them till perhaps next month.

"This coming weekend," said Romaine in a whisper.

"What?" I was shocked to say the least. "What about the premiere?" I felt a little nerdy acknowledging that I followed Romaine's schedule in the press, but it was pretty obvious, anyway.

Romaine giggled. "We staged the premiere to distract from my wedding. I wanted to have a hometown wedding, but I knew the press would get suspicious if all these Hollywood people were showing up in good old Maple Grove. Then they'd storm my backyard and come in with helicopters, and then my wedding would be ruined. So I'm tricking them."

"Wait, there isn't a premiere?" Now I was confused.

"There is, but there's also a wedding the next day."

"Oh!" Now I got it. "That's really smart!" I said. Romaine tapped the side of her head, like she was smart, but then she admitted, "It was my mom's idea."

Samantha came out in her pale green satin bridesmaid dress, and we all oohed and aahed over it. She could have worn a potato sack and still looked like a queen. Her posture was so straight and elegant. Mona got to work on pinning her, and Romaine called her mom over to talk with us.

"Let me grab a pen and paper," I said, and dashed off.

When I came back, Mrs. Ford was saying, "Too complicated!"

"Nothing's too complicated for the Cupcake Club!" I said.

"Well . . . ," said Mrs. Ford. "Romaine and Liam can't agree on flavors, so Romaine was saying it might be cute to do a selection. I think it's too complicated, and it will look messy: chocolate over here, orange here. There needs to be some visual theme or organization."

I nodded. "What's the theme of the wedding? What colors are the tables?"

"Spring colors!" said Romaine, excited. "Pastels. Pale pink, pale blue, pale green, pale yellow."

"Pretty!" I said. "Like the bridesmaids' dresses."

"Exactly!"

I thought for a minute. "Well, we could do white cake and then have different-colored pastel frostings? We could flavor the frostings with some extracts if you wanted. Like the green could be mint, the pink could be raspberry."

Romaine and her mom looked at each other and grinned. "That might be just the thing," said Mrs. Ford. Then she turned to me with a smile, but the look in her eyes was serious. "You can't tell a soul."

"I . . . uh . . ." Can't tell a soul? How am I going to bake cupcakes and not tell the others?

"Pinkie promise!" said Romaine, and she crooked her pinkie at me.

I laughed. "Um . . . the thing is, there are four of us in the Cupcake Club. That's how we work. All together. I can't not tell my partners. I mean, we do all the baking and decorating." I could feel a blush rising from my neck, and my cheeks felt hot. I blinked hard. "I . . . I don't know how I could even bake them all by myself."

Romaine wagged her pinkie at me again. "Come on! You'll figure something out, right?"

Mrs. Ford interjected, "I'm so sorry, honey, but we've found that the more people know, well, the more people tend to find out. We need to keep it between us chickens, or the press will descend and ruin it. And after all our hard work to keep it a secret."

How could I turn down the offer to bake Romaine Ford's wedding cupcakes?

I sighed and crooked my pinkie to link with Romaine's.

"Okay?" She smiled.

"Okay," I said. "I understand." And I did. But I was already dreading keeping a secret like this from my best friends, not to mention how I was ever going to pull this off.

As the morning wore on, the bridal party worked their way though all the dress fittings, as well as two servings of cupcakes each! It was a fun, festive atmosphere the whole time, and I could see Mona relax inch by inch as each member of the party came out in a dress that looked fantastic. Not to be immodest, but I think all the sweets helped keep everyone happy, too.

By the end of the fitting, Mona was in a great mood, and the bridal party was kind of tired and giggly. Romaine got ready for her departure from the store by putting a dark wig on, with sunglasses and a baggy trench coat. It made us all laugh, seeing her like that because she looked so unlike herself.

"Presenting the new *Mrs. Liam Carey!*" announced Samantha, and we all collapsed into giggles. Part of me felt scared for Romaine though, and a little sad. It would be so hard to be stalked by the press the way she is. Then her mom and her sister also donned costumes, as well as Samantha, and they all staggered their departures so that no one would notice them.

Romaine left first, giving me a firm hug, along with her e-mail address, and asking me to send her a proposal as soon as possible. Her mom agreed and suggested a few other flavor ideas, and I made a note of them on my sheet of paper. Samantha also hugged me. "Let's take a photo!" she said, and I almost hugged her. I would have never asked her myself. Patricia took one with my phone, and Samantha was very cute about it. She mimed eating a cupcake with a big grin on her face, and I was laughing. We looked good. I promised not to do anything with the photo until after the wedding. I thought it was so nice how protective Samantha was of Romaine. I'd do the same thing for any of my friends, especially Alexis. Even if she did end up marrying Matt. *Eww . . . ,* I thought. I put that thought out of my head.

By the time they'd all gone, Mona, Patricia, and I collapsed onto the sofas and closed our eyes to rest for a minute. It had been a lot of work and a lot of fun, and we were pooped.

I couldn't stop thinking about Romaine having this fun morning with her family and best friends, and then having to stalk off alone in disguise like a criminal. Now that I'd witnessed some of what she had to go through, I didn't mind that much about not telling my friends about the cupcakes for Romaine's wedding. Even though it would be hard, I would do it for Romaine's sake.

I opened my eyes and stretched. "Well, I'd better go, or I'm going to fall asleep on this sofa."

"I know. Aren't these cushions divine?" asked Mona.

"Divine," I echoed with a giggle.

Mona cracked open an eye and smiled. "Thanks for your help this morning, Emma. You were lovely, as usual."

"It's easy when the clients are so nice."

"I know," agreed Mona. "We're lucky. Now for the rest of the world . . ."

Patricia stood up. "I'll go open up," she said.

I said good-bye to Mona and went to gather my jacket and my cupcake carrier. Patricia paid me for the cupcakes and my time, but I tried to only take the money for the cupcakes.

"It was an honor! A privilege!" I said. "I should be paying you!" I always feel awkward with business transactions. It's why I have an agent for my modeling and why I'm happy to let Alexis handle the Cupcake Club billing and negotiating. I felt a twinge thinking of how I'd have to do it all without her for the wedding cupcakes. Ugh.

"Emma, take the money. I can't have to fight to pay you ever time you come to work here, you silly goose," said Patricia, pressing the envelope into my hand. "Look at Romaine and Samantha and how successful they've been. Don't you think those two ladies know what their work is worth? How do you think they got so far?"

"I guess," I said awkwardly.

"Don't undervalue yourself, sweetie," Patricia said, coming from behind the counter to put her arm around me and walk me to the door. "You're a professional, and you're worth every penny you make, if not more, okay?"

"Thanks," I said, giving her a quick hug. "See you next week!" I lowered my voice to a whisper. "Wedding weekend!"

"Shh!" said Patricia with a wink.

Outside the store, I set out for the pickup area where my dad was waiting for me in the minivan. It was only short walk down the open main stairway and out the front doors of the mall below. I hadn't gotten ten feet from the front of the store, though, when a nice-looking young man said, "Excuse me! Miss!"

On instinct I turned around and slowed down a little, still heading for the stairs. My parents had always told me about not talking to strangers. I saw Dad in the car and gave a little wave, so he could see me. I could see him start to get out of the car. The man looked at him and waved.

"Hi, miss. John Cohane from *Celebrity* magazine. I just saw you exiting The Special Day. I wonder, could you please confirm for me that is where Romaine Ford's wedding dress came from?" He flashed a charming grin at me.

He'd said everything so fast, it took me a minute to process. *Celebrity* magazine? I stood stupidly frozen for a split second, then I realized what was happening, and I turned on my heel and started walking again, fast. I reached the top of the stairs and started jogging down them at a quick clip. He followed me.

"Miss! I'm not looking for a quote or a photo

or anything, just a confirmation? For *Celebrity* magazine."

I was nearly sprinting now, but he was keeping up with me. I couldn't think of anything to say to get him away from me. I thought if I opened my mouth, I might give something away, but I felt like such a loser being mute.

I was scared and wished I could think of something clever to say to get this guy away from me.

My dad took a look at the guy keeping pace with me, and my fear and anger must've been written all over my face, because he came running around the front of the car and yelled, "Hey! You! Back off! You stay away from my daughter right now!" I had only heard him yell like that a few times, and it surprised me.

The reporter looked over in surprise. He put up his hands in the universal *I surrender* pose as I bolted into the back of the car.

"What the heck is going on here?" my dad asked, wheeling to face me.

"He's a reporter. From *Celebrity* magazine. He wanted to know about Romaine Ford's wedding dress." I punched the door's close button, and the door began to slide shut.

"Stay away from us! And get a life!" yelled my

dad. I hadn't seen him so mad in ages.

Luckily, the reporter turned on his heel and quick marched back into the mall. My dad was muttering and returned to the front seat and shut his door.

"That guy had a lotta nerve!" he growled. "Chasing a child!"

I was shaking a little now. That had been scary, and it all happened so fast.

"I . . . I didn't know what to say . . . I was tongue-tied!" I said. I felt embarrassed.

"Good. I'm glad you didn't say a thing to that guy. You know you never, ever talk to strangers, and you always run and yell, like we taught you." My dad looked at me in the rearview mirror. "I'm sorry that happened to you, sweetie. You did the right thing. Exactly the right thing. Never talk to strangers. And especially not to the press. And especially not about Romaine Ford. Mona and Romaine both trust you, and you always have to be true to your word." He raked his fingers through his hair and took a deep breath. "I can't wait till this whole premiere thing blows over. It's ruining this town."

"I know," I agreed, and looked out the window. *And it's not just a premiere . . . ,* I added silently.

CHAPTER 4

Know-It-Alls

I couldn't wait for my mom to get home from Matt's game that morning. I was totally on edge, dying to talk to someone about the morning but completely unable to talk to my friends about it. Thank goodness I had no plans with them for the rest of the day or I would have burst.

Finally, I heard her car in the driveway, and I bolted down from my room, where I'd been practicing my flute, and careened out the back door to see her.

"Emma! My heavens! Is everything okay?" she said, spying me in my socks and cozy pants out in the driveway.

Matt clambered out of the front seat in his baseball uniform and looked me up and down from head to toe, then just shook his head and walked inside.

"Mom!" I whispered loudly.

"What?" she whispered loudly back with a grin. She shut her car door and came around the back to me.

"Mom, be serious! I have to talk to you!" I said.

"Here?" she said, looking around. "Is the house bugged?"

I sighed. "When you are ready to be serious, then we can talk." I tapped my socked foot on the blacktop.

My mom threw her arm around me and gave me a sideways squeeze. "I'm sorry, Emmy. You're just being so funny. What's up?"

"Mom, I've got to tell you something I'm not allowed to tell anyone!"

My mom looked mock-offended. "I'm not anyone? Gee, thanks!"

Finally, I blurted it all out in one sentence without stopping. "Mom, Romaine Ford is getting married next Saturday, and she's asked me to do the cupcakes instead of a wedding cake, but I can't tell anyone, and now I have to do it all by myself!"

"Whaaaaat?"

I stared at her without blinking. She'd heard me right. I wondered what she would say.

"Oh, honey, that is so exciting! Congratulations!" My mom clapped her hands in celebration, but I didn't really feel like celebrating. I was too stressed.

"But, Mom, I can't even tell my friends!"

"Oh, I'm sure it wouldn't matter if you just told . . ."

"I'm not allowed!" I practically yelled. "That's the problem. If word gets out, it could ruin the whole thing!"

I explained to her about Romaine being stalked by the press (I'd decided to wait to tell her about my run-in with the press because she would really freak out) and about how Romaine had specifically staged the premiere here to cover up the wedding and how all she'd ever wanted was a private backyard wedding in her mom's garden.

"Oh, that is so sweet and romantic!" said my mom, her eyes all wistful.

"Yeah, and I can't be the one to wreck it," I said.

"Hmm," said my mom. "Well, I can help you with the order!"

"Thanks. It might come to that. I mean, no offense, but I wish it was my friends. I'm not even sure how to price these cupcakes, never mind make them all by myself."

"Are they elaborate?" she asked.

"Mmm . . . well, I think we're going to do a plain white cake but different-colored pastel frostings. Maybe each with a different flavor."

"Pretty!" said my mom.

"Yeah. Not too hard in terms of assembly. Just a little time-consuming to do all those mini batches of frosting. And she needs more than a hundred of them all together. Ten dozen. I want them to look perfect, though. And Mia and Katie usually do the decorating."

"Wow. A hundred and twenty cupcakes?"

I nodded and watched a beagle mix named Skipper, one of my dog-walking clients, taking a walk across the street with my neighbor. I sighed. Walking dogs was an easier way to make money than baking for celebrity weddings.

"So what's your next step?" asked my mom.

I sighed. "I need to do a pricing e-mail and contract for Romaine and send it out to her today. I'll just use an old sample of Alexis's and kind of cut and paste it."

My mom nodded. "Smart. Okay. Well, let me know if I can help."

"Thanks. I feel better already just having some-one to talk to about it. I'd like you to read over the e-mail before I send it, okay?"

"Sure. Can we go inside now? I'm dying for a cup of coffee!"

I laughed. "Let's go."

That afternoon I struggled over the e-mail and finally came up with a draft that looked okay. Even though I called Romaine by her first name in person, Mom said I should address her by her last name in the e-mail. It said:

Dear Ms. Ford,
Thank you for your interest in Cupcake
Club cupcakes for your event. We propose
baking ten dozen white cupcakes, frosted
in an assortment of six pastel frostings,
each lightly flavored with an extract
of your choice (suggestions include:
lemon, raspberry, lavender, lime, orange,
blueberry, and so forth).
Frosted cupcakes will be delivered for
assembly by the Cupcake Club onto
platters at the Ford Residence at _____
a.m. on Saturday, May 4.

Pricing will be $300.00. (That's still only
$2.50 a cupcake—a bargain!)
Payment due upon receipt of cupcakes,
please.
Many thanks for your continued business.
All the best,
Emma Taylor
The Cupcake Club
(555) 555-2129

I printed out the e-mail and trotted downstairs
for my mom to review it again. She thought it
looked great, so I went back upstairs and sent it.
And then I sat at my computer and stared at my
in-box for twenty minutes, hoping for a response.

I was nervous. Three hundred dollars was a lot
of money, but it was a big and stressful job to do
alone, and part of the price was for my silence.

Most of all I hated not being able to tell my
friends. I felt like a traitor doing business as the
Cupcake Club alone. It was probably illegal, now
that I thought about it. Well, I could tell them all
after the fact and then hand over the money to
Alexis. That made me feel better.

I was dying to hear back from Romaine, but
I finally decided busy celebrities might not even

answer their own e-mail, and it was a weekend, after all. I sighed and put my computer to sleep and went downstairs to watch baseball with my brothers. If you can't beat 'em, join 'em.

At dinner my dad told my mom about the reporter who had chased me, and my mom was shocked it hadn't been the first thing I'd told her.

"I didn't want you to not let me make the cupcakes," I admitted with a shrug.

"What cupcakes?" asked Jake in confusion.

"Oh, it's a long story," I said, and I widened my eyes at my mom to signal that she couldn't say anything.

Luckily, she got the message and nodded. "Well, you did the right thing, Em. The press can be very aggressive and you can see just from that little taste how hard it is for Romaine to preserve any semblance of privacy in her life."

I nodded and took a sip of my milk.

"Any news?" asked my mom.

I shook my head. "I'll check after dinner."

"News about what?" asked Jake.

"Long story," I said again, and Jake sighed in exasperation.

"Why doesn't anyone ever tell me anything?"

"'Cause you're the baby," I said, and I patted him on the head.

"Am not!" he said indignantly.

"Okay, kids," said my dad.

"May I be excused?" I asked.

"Yes, you may," my mom said, and I dashed up to my computer.

There in my in-box was a reply from Romaine! It said:

Hi, Emma—
Thanks for the contract. Everything looks great. Still need your guarantee of confidentiality—please don't tell your friends. I know it will be hard for you, but I think I might have an idea to help. Will be in touch tomorrow to discuss. Sleep well!
Xx, Ro
PS No need to do a tasting. I totally trust your judgment. ☺

Wow! "Xx, Ro"! Now I felt like we were really friends. People would die if they knew Romaine and I were e-mailing each other. This was pretty cool. I imagined the look on Olivia Allen's face— she's kind of a frenemy of mine—and smiled, imagining her reaction if I told her I was helping Romaine Ford with her wedding. I sighed. It was just too bad I couldn't tell my friends. And that they wouldn't be able to help me. How would I pull this off? I shut down my computer with a pit in my stomach and went to take a shower. Sleep well? I didn't think so.

As soon as I woke up the next day I checked my e-mail and my cell phone, but there was no new info from "Ro." The pit in my stomach grew minute by minute as I realized I'd have to face my friends at school and not tell them about seeing Romaine on Saturday or about her wedding and the cupcakes I'd be baking for it.

At my locker the next morning, I avoided eye contact with everyone. I was just hoping I'd get home to find an e-mail from Romaine with some brilliant plan that would keep my friends happy and give me a little relief from carrying these secrets all alone.

Unfortunately, Olivia Allen was walking by and stopped to talk to Kim Walker at the locker across from mine.

"OMG! I heard Romaine Ford is already in town and that Liam Carey is coming tomorrow and is staying at the Stanhope Hotel! We should go stake it out!" Olivia was squealing.

I gulped and willed myself to be silent.

"Totally! Let's go after school!" agreed Olivia's friend Bella.

Olivia continued, "I heard Romaine and Liam are eloping to Tahiti. Isn't that soooo romantic? That's *just* what I would do if I were her. You know, my mom's friend works in a bridal salon, and she said Romaine's wearing a Vera Wang dress in palest pink for the wedding. . . ."

I gritted my teeth. Olivia Allen is such a know-it-all, and she's almost always wrong, wrong, wrong! I wanted to turn around, throttle her, and yell, "She's not eloping! She's getting married right here, this Saturday, in a white Jaden Sacks dress from The Special Day!" It was all I could do to keep my mouth shut.

I slammed my locker door extra hard, though, right as Mia came up alongside me. "Whoa, tiger!" She laughed. "Everything okay?"

I rolled my eyes in the direction of Olivia and motioned that we should walk away. Mia followed. "What's up?" she whispered.

Once we'd gotten halfway down the hall, I exploded. "Olivia Allen is such a know-it-all! It's always a bragathon with her about how much she knows and what an insider she is! It makes me crazy!"

Mia nodded. "I agree. Totally. What was it this time?"

I sighed heavily. I couldn't tell Mia anything, so my hands were kind of tied. I needed to be vague. "Just . . . she thinks she knows everything about Romaine Ford. It just bugs me."

"And you really do know her, so it must be doubly annoying!" said Mia.

I looked at her sideways to make sure she was being serious. Suddenly, I had the feeling that maybe people thought I was as bad as Olivia!

"Wait, do people think I'm annoying about Romaine?" I asked urgently.

Mia looked at me in surprise. "What? No! Not at all! The opposite! You're always so closemouthed about it. Romaine Ford could be at your *house* and you wouldn't tell anyone!"

"Okay, ha-ha." I fake-laughed a little because Mia had kind of hit the nail on the head. "Phew. I just don't want you guys to think I'm, like, possessive of her or something."

Mia shook her head vehemently. "No. Totally not. In fact, most of the time we wish you'd tell us more! You kind of keep it all to yourself."

We'd stopped outside the English classroom where Mia was heading; I was walking on to social studies. "Is that bad?" I asked.

"No, we understand. It just leaves us hungry for more! We just sometimes wish you could trust your best friends enough to tell us. We *can* keep a secret, you know." Mia laughed. "Bye!"

"Okay," I said weakly. "Bye."

"We understand"? "We can keep a secret"? That means they've been talking about me, I thought as I continued down the hall. My best friends have been talking about me and Romaine Ford, and they understand my secrecy but wish I'd tell them more. Oh boy.

And it was only about to get worse. Way worse.

CHAPTER 5

Major

At lunch I ducked into the library and checked my e-mail. Sure enough, there was an e-mail from Romaine:

> Hey, Em—
> What if we hire the CC to bake cupcakes for the premiere on Friday night? Say ten dozen. Something jazzy. That way you can include them in something and not feel like you totally left them out. You can bill me directly and I'll have the studio pay me back. Let me know.
> Xx, Ro

"OMG!" I said loudly.

"Shh!" warned the librarian with a smile.

"Sorry," I whispered. I quickly exited my e-mail and jumped up, knocking my chair backward in my haste.

I glanced guiltily at the librarian who was now wagging her finger at me. *Sorry!* I mouthed with a shrug as I righted the chair.

She winked and I waved good-bye.

Out in the hall I broke into a run to reach the cafeteria. I fervently hoped the Cupcakers were still there. Luckily, they were!

I ducked through the crowds and beelined for our table.

"Where were you?" asked Katie.

"Are you sitting down?" I asked.

They all laughed because obviously they were.

"I have MAJOR news. MAJOR!"

Their eyes opened wide, and they all began smiling hopefully.

"What?" asked Alexis.

I sat down and said, "Romaine Ford has asked the Cupcake Club to bake ten dozen cupcakes for her premiere on Friday night."

There was a stunned silence, and then the girls started shouting and whooping so much that everyone in the cafeteria turned to stare, but we didn't care.

We jumped up and hugged and danced in place, and I swear I almost cried, I was so overjoyed. It just felt great to be able to share *any* news with my besties. It was a huge relief.

And guess who walked right up to us to ask what was going on? Yup! Olivia Allen!

"What are you people celebrating?" she asked, with a smirk on her face.

I'd already had the joy of delivering the news once, so I turned to my friends as if to say, "You tell."

Katie beamed proudly and said, "We're baking cupcakes for Romaine Ford's movie premiere on Friday!"

Olivia's jaw dropped, and she was speechless. It was so classic; it was right out of a movie. She gulped and stammered, "W-wow. Wow. That is so . . ."

"We know," said Alexis, and turned away to continue celebrating. Olivia staggered away in shock.

We sat back down to talk details, but it was getting toward the end of lunch, and we all had somewhere to be next period.

"Can everyone get together at my house today?" asked Katie. "We need to get cracking!"

We all agreed and stood to go. I'd have to grab a sandwich on our way out and eat it on the way to English, but it was worth it.

Alexis was all dreamy and said, "Can you imagine the exposure for the Cupcake Club? What if we're mentioned in *Celebrity* magazine? You know how they always feature those big celebrity parties?"

We laughed because Alexis was always about the business and our exposure and growth. Then we parted ways, eager to reconvene after school and get cracking, as Katie said. I just hoped I could keep my mouth shut about my other cupcake job. Gulp.

We walked from school to Katie's, brainstorming all the way. It was an unusually gorgeous day—warm and blue-skied, everything smelling great—and it made me happy just to be outside.

"Oh, I hope the weather stays like this for—" OMG. I almost said for Romaine's wedding! Luckily, no one caught my hesitation.

"I know," agreed Katie. "Even though the theater is inside the mall, Romaine would still have to run from her house to the car, so if it rained, it would ruin her hair."

"Yeah," I agreed, digging my palm with my nails

to keep myself from saying any more. Thank goodness Katie had thought I was talking about the premiere.

At Katie's, we gathered around the computer at her mom's desk in the kitchen.

"Okay, the movie, *One Sweet Summer*, is about a woman who owns a candy store and falls in love with this politician who's all about making people eat healthier and wants to make all these new health laws and close down her store," said Alexis as she read from the movie's website. She clicked on the button to watch the trailer and the music started up. Then Romaine came onscreen looking radiant, her blond hair cut shoulder length and swingy. She was dressed in white jeans and a red-and-white–striped sailor's T-shirt—fresh and cute.

"Awww!" said my friends. I smiled, almost proudly.

The trailer went on to show how the handsome but strict politician wanted to shut down Romaine because her store was next to a school and the kids all came in and bought candy every day, and he thought it was making them unhealthy. But then it turned out she was helping kids with homework and giving good life advice and employing some of them and generally being an all-around good anchor for the neighborhood. And, as it turns out, none of the kids spent enough money to be unhealthy because they're all poor; Romaine's candy store is barely staying in business. So the handsome politician turns sweet and falls in love with her, and together they get the kids into eating healthier—I almost had to laugh because it's what my mom says: You can eat treats, but it's all about moderation—and it all ends well.

The trailer finished, and we all sighed happily.

"I can't wait to see it!" said Katie, and we agreed.

"Will we get to see the movie on Friday?" asked Alexis.

"She didn't say anything about that," I said.

"That's okay," said Katie. "We still get to do the cupcakes!"

"So should we do candy-themed cupcakes?" I asked.

"That could be cute," said Mia thoughtfully.

"Or should we focus on the premiere and do something movie-ish?" Katie wondered. "I saw something somewhere. . . ." She typed something into a search engine and pulled up some cute cupcakes with "popcorn" on top, wrapped in retro-striped popcorn bucket papers.

"Oooh!" We all loved them.

"Would they be hard to do?" I asked, leaning over Katie's shoulder and squinting at the screen. "What are they made out of?"

"You take mini marshmallows and snip Xs into them, twist them into kernel shapes, and then mist them with yellow food coloring, so they look buttery."

"And how about the popcorn bucket papers? Is that hard? 'Cause they kind of make it," said Mia.

"These look like a lot of work. I liked Emma's idea—candy-themed cupcakes. Maybe just make some traditional white cupcakes with white frosting and put colorful candies on top?" said Alexis sensibly.

"No, but that will look so amateur!" protested Katie. "What would *Celebrity* magazine say?"

Well, that got Alexis.

"We do need to put our best work forward," she admitted.

"How hard could they be?" asked Mia.

"Do you have any mini marshmallows we could practice with?" I asked.

"No. Why don't I get some supplies tonight with my mom, and we can do a trial baking session tomorrow, back here?"

We agreed that was a good idea.

"It's really just printing out the templates for the wrappers and trimming them, and figuring out how to make the marshmallow popcorn look real," Katie said.

"Right," said Alexis.

"Ten dozen times," I added. Just like the wedding cupcakes . . .

"Once we get the hang of it, it will be really easy," said Mia confidently.

"Okay," we agreed.

We did a little homework, had a snack, and then headed home for the evening. I felt much better about being able to share at least some Romaine info with my friends, but I was still carrying a big secret around with me. And it was about to get worse.

At home, my mom had just come in from work, and she was listening to the voice mail messages. I waved, and she waved back and kept on writing down who she needed to call back. And then there was one for me. It was Mona.

"Hello, darlings. It's Mona!" she trilled on the voice mail. "I'd like to request the help of lovely Emma for Tuesday night. I apologize for the short notice, but we've got final fittings for our friend's bridal party, and I would love Emma's assistance. Please call me back! Hope you can make it, Emma! Kiss, kiss!"

That was the final message. My mom and I smiled at each other.

"Fun!" said my mom.

"I know! But oh! Bummer. I have a Cupcake Club meeting. And guess what?" I relayed the exciting news about the premiere cupcakes.

"Oh, that is so thoughtful of Romaine!" said my mom. "But it doesn't really solve the issue of you baking all those cakes for Saturday by yourself, does it?"

I pursed my lips grimly. "Nuh-uh," I said, shaking my head.

"Well, maybe the boys will help," said my mom. We stared at each other silently for a moment.

Then we both laughed hysterically.

When we finished, we wiped our eyes, and I said, "I guess I'd better tell my friends about tomorrow. Maybe we can push the meeting to Wednesday."

"Okay. Homework?"

"Not much. I did some already."

"Great. Steak on the grill for dinner," said my mom.

"Yum."

Upstairs, I dashed off an e-mail to the gang, telling them I had to help Mona tomorrow night and if we could possibly postpone the meeting until Wednesday. Alexis quickly wrote back that it was fine, but perhaps we ought to start printing and trimming the wrappers in the meantime, which I thought was brilliant. She also asked Katie to send her pricing and quantity estimates, so she could work up a proposal for Romaine that would cover our costs. Katie readily agreed. Phew!

I was glad my friends were so flexible. I called Mona back and told her I could come tomorrow, and she said she'd come by my house and pick me up.

"Hey, have you been bothered by the press?" I asked before we hung up.

"Honey, you have no idea!" said Mona. "They're like bees to honey over here. But I haven't said a peep, and neither has anyone else."

I told her about the guy from *Celebrity* magazine, and she was proud of me for not saying anything. "Those guys are tough," she said. "We'll make sure someone walks you to and from the car next time. You were smart to stay mum."

"It's easy staying mum with a stranger. It's with my friends that are the tough part!"

"I know. It's been hard for me too. Especially because it's pretty exciting for The Special Day!"

It was true. I thought about how excited we were in the cafeteria today and how I was bursting to tell the others about the wedding cupcakes too. I couldn't imagine how hard it would be if I owned my own store and had such an exciting client. It would be impossible to stay quiet.

We hung up with promises to keep silent and said we were looking forward to the next day. I practiced my flute for a little while to use up some energy, then checked my e-mail one last time before I headed back downstairs to help with dinner. There was only one new e-mail. It was from Olivia, and it said, "Can I help with the cupcakes for the premiere?"

Of all the nerve! I groaned and shut off my computer without replying. I needed some steak for energy before tackling this one.

CHAPTER 6

Home Sweet Home

The next morning I checked my e-mail after I'd woken up. Alexis had sent a message with a schedule that said:

> Hi, all—
> How's this:
> Weds.: Sample session
> Thurs.: Bake
> Fri.: Assemble premiere cupcakes & bake minis for Mona
> —A

I wrote back that it looked great and that as soon as she had an estimate, I would forward it to Romaine. "BTW," I added, "Olivia Allen wants to help ☹"

It took only a second for Alexis to reply: "NO WAY!!!!!!!!!" The others quickly followed in the same vein. Oh boy. I sighed. I did not look forward to telling Olivia no.

Later at school, I thought I had avoided Olivia entirely, and as I was leaving school, I was sure I'd made a clean getaway. But then I heard my name being called, and I turned to find her running toward me, a few of her hangers-on following behind her. She came right up to my side and linked her arm though mine, saying, "Are we all set for Friday?"

"Uh . . . um . . . ," I stammered.

Olivia flipped her hair and smiled her boldest smile, looking at her friends who had caught up with us. "Wait, more important, what are you wearing?" she asked.

My stomach dropped. Did she know about the fitting tonight? But how could she? "For what?" I mustered.

Olivia laughed a twinkling fake laugh and swatted me. "The premiere, silly!"

"Oh . . . I . . . We don't get to go to the premiere. We're just baking cupcakes for it. It's not like we're invited."

Olivia's smile dropped instantly, and she unlinked her arm from mine. "Wait, I thought we were all going to the premiere!"

I shook my head and looked at her like she was crazy. "We, the Cupcake Club, are baking cupcakes, dropping them off, and going home. That's all. We were never attending the actual event."

Olivia scowled at me. "Then what were you all so excited for?"

"For our business to get recognition and from that, more clients!"

"OMG, that is so lame. Seriously?"

"Uh . . . yeah! Hello? We've worked really hard on the Cupcake Club, and it's a big deal for us. Maybe our company's name will be in the press."

"What about your names? And photos?"

I shrugged. "I don't care about that." I was about to point out that as a local model, I see my photo in newspapers and magazines plenty, but that would be bragging, and I don't like to do that. (Unfortunately, Olivia often brings out the braggy side of me, which I hate.)

"Wow. That is so lame," Olivia said again, shaking her head as if she were disappointed with me.

"Sorry!" I said, hating myself for apologizing. But inside I was jumping for joy that Olivia had no interest in the event if she wouldn't get to attend it herself. I hadn't even had to tell her no! "Bye," I added, and started to walk away.

"Hey!" called Olivia. I turned back. "How did you get this job, anyway?"

I grinned. "Romaine asked me to do it," I said.

Then I turned again and walked quickly away, giggling as Olivia stood rooted to the spot.

Unlike my usual The Special Day routine, today Mona picked me up at my house rather than my mom dropping me off at the store. Mona was in an unmarked white van, and she looked kind of hilarious behind the wheel—so glamorous and decked out, but driving this big van.

She tooted the horn twice, and I kissed my mom good-bye and ran out. I had eaten a PB&J, so I wouldn't get hungry while I worked, and I was dressed neatly but casually in white jeans, a pale blue T-shirt, and a cute rope belt, with blue-and-white—striped shoes.

Patricia hopped out of the front seat ("You look fabulous!" she said) and slid open the side door, so I could I clamber in and perch on the one bench seats in the back. Behind me was a cargo area with a rolling rack of dresses on it, all pastel colored except for Romaine's big white, puffy one and the junior bridesmaid's simple white one.

"Love the cute outfit! Buckle up, darling!" called Mona as she piloted the big van out of my driveway. Soon we were underway and headed to the far side of town. As we drew into Romaine's neighborhood, the pieces of land got bigger, and the houses were farther apart. It was also hillier, as opposed to the flat area where my friends and I live.

We reached the bottom of a driveway with a white gate, and there was a little call box. I'd driven by here dozens of times, hoping to catch a glimpse of Romaine, but I'd never seen her outside, and you can't see any part of the house from the road. (I've tried.) I was excited to see what it looked like. I knew it would be a huge mansion—maybe with an indoor and outdoor swimming pool and a six-car garage!

Mona pushed the call button, and a voice said, "Hello?"

Mona said, "Special delivery from The Special Day bridal salon!"

Then the voice said, "Hi! Come on up!" The white gates slowly began to swing open. Patricia looked back at me with wide, excited eyes, and I grinned like a maniac.

We started up the hill, and I held my breath until the mansion came into sight. After a curve or two in the driveway, we came to . . . a medium-size white house. It was very pretty, but honestly it didn't look all that different from my house.

"This must be the guest house," I said knowledgably.

"Actually . . . ," Mona began.

The front door flew open, and Romaine was there waving, with buttery yellow light spilling out from behind her and illuminating the porch, where a white wooden swing hung from chains and some white wicker furniture was casually arranged around a coffee table.

Mona eased the van up the hill and into the parking area by the back door where a basketball net stood over the blacktop play area next to a garage. There was an old blue SUV parked there, with all kinds of hockey and lacrosse stickers plastered across the back. I recognized the logo from one of Sam's teams on one of the stickers. I craned my neck to see the rest of the house from out of the car's window.

"Wait, this is it?" I asked incredulously. "It isn't a mansion?"

"Well, it's a beautiful house!" declared Mona.

"A lovely family home," agreed Patricia.

I tried to hide my disappointment. "Oh. I thought . . ."

Romaine came bounding over to the van in sneakers and work-out clothes. "Not what you were expecting, I bet, after that security gate!" She laughed. "This is where I grew up. My parents refuse to move! We had to get the gate because of the press. Sorry."

"I wouldn't move either, darling," said Mona smoothly. "It's divine. Just divine."

Romaine giggled. "Yeah, with my brothers' and sisters' height chart on the kitchen's doorframe, and the front door scratched up from our puppy, who's now six, and bunk beds in the attic guest room . . ."

"It's home," said Patricia definitively.

"And a beautiful home it is," added Mona.

Romaine sighed, and for the first time I saw that she might be nervous or embarrassed to have us at her house, just like anyone would be. "It's true. For better or for worse." Then she giggled again. "Listen to me, I'm already in wedding mode! Come on in!"

Mona, Patricia, and I unloaded the van and began ferrying the dresses, shoes, and accessories into Romaine's family room. Florence helped us, and it was done in no time flat. Mrs. Ford offered us drinks and cookies, but we declined and got down to business. It was time to talk about the wedding.

"Now let me show you how this all will work," began Mona as she gestured to the items for Mrs. Ford, Romaine, and Florence. "Everyone has a color, and it is all coded on this chart." She handed a laminated sheet to Mrs. Ford. "Each person's shoes, dress, and any other accessories—like the veil, in your case, Romaine—are color coded with a sticker on the outside of their box or dress bag. See?" She gestured to Florence's dress, with its pale green sticker, then to a nearby shoe box, again with the pale green sticker, and finally to a clear plastic tub that held a hair clip and the green sticker on the outside. "The number of items per person are noted next to her name and color. For example, you can see Florence only has three items and here they all are."

"Wow," Romaine said breathlessly.

"This is so fabulous. Just amazing. I am very impressed," said Mrs. Ford, looking up with a big smile. "Thank you."

"Yes, thank you so much!" said Romaine.

Mona beamed proudly, and Patricia and I joined in.

Mona continued, "Now, the morning of the

wedding, I will be here at nine a.m. sharp and will help everyone into their dresses. I will be at your disposal for any last-minute alterations and Patricia will be here with our store's car, and she can dash anywhere we need to pick up anything. We will have extra stockings, no-slip pads for the shoes, hankies, stain remover—our usual emergency kit. Not that there will be any emergencies, of course! Just know we are prepared for anything."

"Great," said Romaine. "The wedding starts at twelve thirty, so they want us dressed for photos by eleven. Hair and makeup are coming at . . . ugh . . . seven thirty, so they can do everyone."

"And, of course, the caterers will be crawling all over, setting things up, and the tent . . . ," added Mrs. Ford.

"And the cupcakes will be arriving!" Romaine said, smiling in my direction.

I smiled back, nodding, but I gulped nervously at the same time. Now that I was in the middle of it, I was feeling like maybe it hadn't been so smart to accept this big-league job, and all on my own, too. But it was too late to back out now. The wedding was only four days away! Oh boy. I felt nauseated all of a sudden. What had I gotten myself into?

I caught Mona's eye and saw her looking at me

with a concerned look on her face. Her brows were knitted together with worry. But then she quickly smoothed away the expression and looked happily and expectantly at Mrs. Ford.

Mrs. Ford said, "Why don't I show you around, so you have the lay of the land. That way you won't need me on Saturday morning, since I'll be running around like a chicken with my head cut off!"

We followed Mrs. Ford on a tour of the house. It was very pretty and very comfortable. It was larger than my house or those of my friends, and it had bigger rooms and was more "decorated," but not over-the-top at all. The living room and family room had coordinated upholstery on the furniture, with pretty printed fabric and coordinating throw pillows. There was bright lighting everywhere, which created a nice homey feel. The kitchen had new appliances and was all crisp and white and clean. She showed us the backyard and the long sweep of grass where the tent was being put up tomorrow and the tree with the swing where Liam had proposed to Romaine. The garden had hot-pink peonies in bloom, and the pale purple lilacs along the back of the house perfumed the air with a gorgeous, sweet scent. I looked at the yard and thought it was the perfect spot to get married.

Romaine still shared a room with her sister upstairs, and they still had their awards from camp and cheerleading all around, plus a poster from her school play when Romaine was the star. *Eat your heart out,* Celebrity *magazine!* I wanted to yell. And *How do you like this, Olivia Allen?* But of course I didn't. I just stayed quiet as Mrs. Ford explained where the bridal party would be getting dressed (in Romaine's other sister's room) and where Romaine would be getting ready (in the master bedroom), and she and Mona discussed in what order and timing they should do it all.

"I can't believe this is all really happening!" Romaine said to me, girlish and sweet as the "adults" took care of the details. "I've been looking forward to it for so long. I can't believe I'll get to be Mrs. Liam Carey after this weekend! It's so amazing!"

"When does your fiancé get here?" I asked. I didn't want to pry, but I felt like I could reveal at least a small amount of my huge enthusiasm for the event.

Romaine sighed happily. "Tomorrow. We're going to sneak over to Green Lake for a private dinner at his friend's restaurant. Just the two of us! I hope we can pull it off."

I winced, thinking of the reporter stalking little old me. "I hope so too. That would be a nice start to the weekend."

"It's going to be so wild having his family here, and our closest friends, all together in one place— the people we love the most! This is why I wanted to do a backyard wedding, with a sit-down lunch. Having it here made the choices obvious because the numbers had to be small. That's why we're only having a hundred guests for the lunch."

A hundred people still sounded like a lot to me. Especially if you were making cupcakes for all of them. "I totally get it," I said. "It's going to be great. What are you serving for the meal?"

Romaine described a luncheon that included Liam's favorite (chicken curry with rice and chutney) and hers (filet of beef with horseradish cream sauce on the side); green salad; skinny green beans; roasted potatoes with shallots; amazing rolls and breads with a cheese platter; and the cupcakes (my cupcakes!), with small platters of handmade chocolates shipped in from her cousin's sweets store in Portland, Oregon.

"Yum! That sounds soooo delicious!" I said. My mouth was watering. "I think I'd like to have lunch in my backyard for my wedding too."

71

Romaine nodded happily. "It's perfect. We might have a big blowout at some nightclub when we get back to LA, invite all the people we have to, let the press in. But this Saturday will just be for us."

"Fun," I said, and we smiled happily at each other.

"Now you understand why I need your silence," she said.

"I always understood," I replied. It was true.

"Thanks," said Romaine. "I really appreciate it."

And I knew she did. I just hadn't known how hard it would be to actually follow.

CHAPTER 7

Never Enough Hours in the Day

We were at the Fords' for about an hour and a half—Mona did a final fitting on Romaine's dress on the spot—and then it was time to go. We left everything neatly organized but out of the way, and Mona and Patricia promised they were on call until the event.

"See you Friday with the movie cupcakes," said Romaine. "And I'll see you some time Saturday morning, right?" said Romaine.

"Yup! Can't wait!" I agreed.

Once we were safely in the van and out of the Fords' driveway, Mona looked at me in the rear-view mirror and said, "Okay, tell the truth: What's up with the cupcakes for Saturday?"

"I . . . What . . . Wait . . ." I was speechless.

Mona grinned. "I knew it! I could tell by that funny look you got on your face when Romaine mentioned the cupcakes that something was up. Tell me everything."

I figured it'd be okay to tell Mona and Patricia about the cupcakes since they already knew about the wedding. So I took a deep breath and explained to them as we drove back to my house about the ten dozen pastel-colored cupcakes Romaine expected for Saturday and how I'd have to bake, frost, and box them all on my own late on Friday night and on Saturday morning and how I couldn't tell any of my friends and I felt dishonest doing business as the Cupcake Club when it was just me and how we now had these premiere cupcakes to do too, and so on and so on. By the time I finished, we'd been sitting in my driveway for five minutes and my mom had come out to make sure everything was okay. I'd waved her back in and said I'd be right along.

At the end of the telling, I sighed, and so did Mona and Patricia.

"Well, that is complicated," agreed Patricia.

"Let me think about this overnight. I bet we can come up with a plan to help you," said Mona.

"Thanks," I said. "I think I can do it, but it's just a lot. And I hate keeping secrets from my friends.

Also, I don't want to do a bad job, you know?"

"Running a business is very complicated; as much as I enjoy being on my own, it helps to have confidantes and coworkers to bounce things off. I can't imagine doing it alone. Listen, I'll call you in the morning. You're not alone. And thanks for your help tonight," said Mona, sliding a white envelope from The Special Day to me.

"Mona! I didn't do anything! You can't pay me to take a tour of Romaine Ford's childhood home. I should be paying you!"

"Stop this silliness. I've never met anyone like you. You never want any of my money. Come on. Take it!" She flapped the envelope at me.

Patricia nodded. "Go on."

I sighed heavily and took the envelope.

"That's my girl!" said Mona with a cackle. "Never forget you're a businesswoman! Don't sell yourself short!"

"Thanks. And thank you for taking me. It was a really fun night and a major privilege. I was proud to be there with you two."

"We were proud to have you, darling!" said Mona, and then to Patricia, "Isn't she divine?"

"Just divine." Patricia smiled, and I got out of the van.

❁

The next morning I had an e-mail from Mona. "Call me, darling. I have a brilliant idea!"

I could hardly resist from calling, but it was only six thirty, so it would have to wait until at least lunchtime.

At our lockers that morning, Katie told me she had all the supplies for the premiere samples and we should meet at the bike rack after school to go to Alexis's house for our baking session. She was so excited and happy and nice about it. My tongue hurt where I had to bite it, so I wouldn't tell her about my evening at Romaine Ford's house. It was eating me up inside to keep all this incredible news a secret from my best friends. I felt like a traitor— like someone I didn't even know. How could I be doing this?

At lunch I snuck into the girls' bathroom and managed a call to Mona.

"Emma, darling! Why do you sound like you're calling me from the train station?"

I laughed. "I'm in the bathroom at school!"

"Then I'll make this quick. Tell your friends I need ten dozen cupcakes for an event Saturday morning. We can route the billing through me— everything. Just follow the specifications Romaine gave to you, and you can even deliver them here if you'd like, early though, because we'll be leaving by eight thirty to go to the Fords'."

"Oh, Mona!" I breathed a huge sigh of relief. "That is a perfect idea."

"I realize you still can't tell your friends the complete truth, but this is better than nothing, yes?"

"Yes! Thank you! I've got to run. I'll talk to you soon!"

I was flooded with relief at the idea of sharing this new cover story with the Cupcakers. Now they could help me and I wouldn't have to do it all alone or risk coming up with some dumb lie.

I left the stall and who was standing there but Olivia Allen, slowly washing her hands and looking at me in the mirror.

"Good news?" she asked finally.

Frantically, I replayed my end of the conversation in my mind. Had I given anything away? I didn't think so. Oh boy. I decided I'd better wash my hands too, which I did quickly and without making any more eye contact with Olivia.

But still, as I left, Olivia said, "Good luck," (not that nicely, by the way) and began applying clear lip gloss. The whole encounter left me rattled.

And yet again I found myself at lunch with

big news to deliver to the Cupcake Club.

"Ready?" I began.

"Oh boy," joked Mia. "What's next? Romaine Ford's wedding cake?"

"Ha-ha." I laughed weakly. OMG. *How did she guess that right off the bat?* "No, just a big job from Mona. Very exciting. Great exposure," I added meaningfully as I looked at Alexis. She nodded like an executive waiting at a boardroom table for the underling to begin her presentation, which is what I felt like.

"So what is it?" asked Katie excitedly.

I plastered a smile on my face. "Instead of her usual order of mini cupcakes, Mona needs ten dozen regular cupcakes Saturday morning for a huge bridal event she's having. Easy, breezy: white cake, pastel frosting, a few with mild flavorings, like lemon or raspberry. Great, right?"

But everyone just stared at me blankly.

Finally, Alexis said, "Well, you explained we can't do it, right? And why, of course?"

"Why did Mona wait until the eleventh hour to ask us this?" asked Katie in confusion. "She's usually so organized."

"Uh . . . I," I said. "I think it was kind of a spontaneous thing. . . . It just . . . came together."

"Ten dozen cupcakes doesn't sound spontane-ous!" said Mia. "Do you think we might have been her backup? Like someone else fell through?"

I turned back to Alexis. "Wait, what do you mean we can't do it?" I said.

"There's no way we can get all that work done—not if we want fresh cupcakes . . . ," said Alexis.

"Or pretty ones!" added Katie

"I'm sure we could charge whatever we need to, uh, get the job done?" I asked.

"That's not the point," said Alexis slowly. "We still have to go to school on Friday. There's just not enough hours in the day."

"But Mona's our best client!" I protested. Now I was starting to feel panicky. If the Cupcake Club didn't agree to do this baking with me, I was back to doing it all alone—and in defiance of the club's decision to decline the job!

"I know, but she's not really playing by the rules," said Alexis, cool as a cucumber. I wanted to throttle her right then, even if she is my best friend.

"Listen, I have a good relationship with Mona, and I don't want to ruin it. We were going to have to do her minis for this week, anyway. This is just a slightly larger order. What if . . . what if I come up with a plan, a larger workforce, to help us get this done? Would you agree to that? We could do it at my house."

The other three looked at one another and shrugged.

"I guess?" said Mia. "How many people could you possibly pull in?"

"And when?" asked Alexis.

"Just trust me. Let me see what I can organize tonight," I said grimly.

"We'll still meet up for the after-school baking session today in the meantime," said Katie.

"Right," we all agreed, and we headed our separate ways to class.

At Alexis's house, no one made mention of the cupcakes for Mona. It was like they definitely weren't happening unless I figured out a way to make everything work. It made me really mad. After all, here I was, dropping this movie premiere job in everyone's lap . . . I was the one who got us this job, after all, and it was a concession, anyway! We wouldn't even be doing it if I hadn't agreed to bake the wedding cupcakes! They had the chance to bake the wedding cupcakes themselves, and they were too stubborn or lazy to do it. Granted, they didn't know what they were turning down, but why should I have to tell them? Mona was our best and more regular client. If there was anyone we should be doing a favor for, it was her!

I mostly stayed silent as Katie demonstrated how to twist and pull the mini marshmallows together to form lumpy-looking popcorn. Mia, meanwhile, sprayed the lumps with the yellow food coloring, and Alexis was trimming the striped popcorn bag papers. None of it was that hard; it was just time-consuming. And the truth was, it didn't look as amazing as it had in the photos. I didn't dare say anything, but I wondered if the others were thinking it too.

After about an hour of work had only produced a stack of around fifteen papers and ten lumps of "popcorn," I said, "Are we sure we want to do this design? It seems slow going."

Everyone turned to look at me.

"Well, we're doing the prep now. We'll have time. We can store the marshmallows in Tupperware and just assemble the cupcakes on Friday afternoon," said Katie.

"When are we baking them?" I asked.

"It will have to be tomorrow, after school," she replied.

Alexis smacked her forehead. "I need to do a

run to the bake shop and get some more bulk sugar and flour tonight. Oh, I hope my mom can take me."

"Make sure you get enough for . . ." I almost said "Romaine's cupcakes." I caught myself in time. "Mona's . . ."

Alexis sighed. "I don't know if we're even doing those, and you know I don't like to carry such a big inventory of dry goods; they get stale so fast. We just don't need that much flour sitting around if we're not sure we're doing the job, you know?" She looked at me kind of defiantly.

"We're doing it," I said firmly.

The others exchanged uneasy looks.

"Look, Em, why don't you walk us through the timeline? How do you could see us doing this?" Alexis asked.

I took a deep breath. "Okay, we do the popcorn and paper trimming tonight. As much as we can, I guess. Then tomorrow night we bake; at my house would be easiest, since we'll keep everything in one place for assembly and delivery. Friday afternoon we assemble the popcorn cupcakes and start to bake . . . Mona's cupcakes. Friday night after the premiere we finish baking Mona's cupcakes. Then Saturday morning we frost and deliver."

"And we deliver to the premiere when?" asked Alexis.

"Six o'clock on Friday."

"And when do we make the pastel-colored frostings?" asked Katie, her face scrunched up. At least she looked like she was trying to make it work rather than catch me in some harebrained scheme, which was what Alexis was doing.

"Look, I'm not an idiot! We've been in tight spots before. We can do this. We won't have a lot of time to hang around the premiere. We'll need to get home to keep working but . . ." I caught the girls exchanging uneasy looks. "Wait . . . ," I said. "Is this all because you want to go to the premiere? Seriously? We're not even invited!"

Mia burst in, wailing, "I know! But we want to at least look great and watch all the stars file in!"

"It's such an opportunity! We could bring our cameras! Get autographs!" agreed Katie.

I looked at Alexis. She shrugged and looked away, like she was embarrassed to admit it. "Guys," I said. "We're going to the premiere as professionals. Sure, we can linger for a little bit and see who's there, but we've got to get back to work. Come on. Alexis, you of all people should understand!"

"But Trent Channing will be there!" she cried.

"OMG," I said, and I put my head in my hands and shook it from side to side. I can't compete with Trent Channing. But maybe there was someone who could. . . .

CHAPTER 8

All Hands on Deck

$\mathcal{M}$att, I am not kidding. I will literally *pay* you. I will do *anything*! I'll give you whatever you want! Seriously! Please!"

Matt was looking at me with a glint in his eye as his feet rested on my desk. He was tipped back in my chair, with his hands locked behind his head, and as he surveyed my room, I knew what was coming next.

"This," he said finally.

"Oh, Matt."

I'm the only one with a good bedroom. Matt and Sam share, and it drives them both crazy. (Sam is a slob and Matt is neat. Or maybe it's the other way around. I can never tell. It always looks gross in there to me.) Jake sleeps in a former tiny closet that my mom keeps saying is going to stunt his growth. Since I'm the only girl, I have a glorious bedroom redone by my mom and me, and everyone in the house wants it.

"What? You said anything!" He thunked the chair legs back down to the floor and stood up to leave. "I guess you weren't serious!"

"Okay! Okay! Fine. You can move in here. I'll take . . . Jake's room, and Jake can move in with Sam. But you can't change anything. I want the opportunity to win it back within six months, okay? Deal?" I put out my hand, and Matt stared down at it for what seemed like an eternity. Finally, he reached out and shook it.

"Deal," he said.

"But you have to also bring George Martinez and at least one other cute friend. Not some weirdo loser. Got it?"

"Fine," he said, but he clearly wasn't listening. He wandered off. "I've got to go get my tape measure. You're welcome!" he called over his shoulder.

I looked around my room and shuddered. What had I just done?

I booted up my computer. Then I began pecking out an e-mail. It said:

Hey, Olivia—
In case you change your mind about
helping with the cupcakes for the premiere,
we are going to deliver them ourselves
and stay to watch the celebs file in. We
should have a good spot to watch them.
You can help make the cupcakes with us
after school on Friday, but the only catch is,
we need you to come back and help with
another huge order after the premiere. We'll
give you your share of the profits. In?
Emma

Then I winced and pushed send. Now it was time to e-mail the others.

Hey—
Matt, George Martinez, and one other
hottie, plus maybe Olivia Allen (sorry, but
she offered) are coming to help on Friday.
Now can we say yes? Let me know, please,
so Mona doesn't have to wait. Thanks.

It was kind of a sharply worded e-mail, and I knew it was weak of me to play on Katie's crush on George and Alexis's crush on Matt, but I needed to use whatever I had to get this done. It was the only way. I went down to dinner before I'd heard back from anyone, and when I came back, there were two replies—one from Olivia and one from Alexis. Coincidentally, they both had written just one word: "Fine."

"Woo-hoo!" I whooped, which was pathetic when you think about it. But oh well. At least we'd get this done.

I finished my homework and grimly set to the task of trimming dozens of popcorn wrappers for the premiere cupcakes. It was midnight before I went to sleep, and I'd only done sixteen.

At school the next day, Olivia was bragging it up about the premiere in front of her friends.

"Emma, where are you having your hair done for the event?" she asked dramatically.

"Oh . . . uh, in my bathroom?" I said. I refused to play her game.

"Someone's coming to you? That is so chic! Who?"

I rolled my eyes. "Olivia, we are going to the premiere to work. Yes, it is true that I am friendly with Romaine Ford, but she will most likely not even be there when we're there. We will make the cupcakes, deliver them, perhaps stay for a few minutes to see if we can spot some stars, and then we head back to work. The big stars don't come until the very last minute, I'm sure."

"Oh, Emma. Such a worker bee!"

I turned to find Alexis standing behind me with an unhappy look on her face. She disliked Olivia even more than I did, and tomorrow was not going to be pleasant for her.

"One thing I was wondering . . . ," said Alexis. "Do you have the ride organized to the premiere?"

"Oh, yes. My dad is taking us," I said.

"In the minivan?" asked Alexis.

"Yeah," I said. *Is there something wrong with that? I wanted to ask.*

But Alexis nodded. "Good. Just wanted to make sure we have enough room for everyone," she said, looking disdainfully at Olivia.

I grinned. "Or were you hoping we might not?" I asked.

Alexis—still my best friend even though I was aggravated with her—grinned back. "Mind reader," she said, and we laughed.

After school we raced to my house to begin baking. Alexis's mom had dropped off all the supplies late last night, and there were huge tubs of butter, sacks of sugar and flour, and dozens and dozens of eggs. It's a good thing we have a backup fridge in our garage. It's usually filled with gallons of milk for the boys, but my mom made room, so we were set.

Alexis had also bought a new kit of food coloring, yellow spray "mist" for the popcorn coloring, and an assortment of extracts to flavor the frosting for "Mona's" cupcakes.

I pulled out my pride and joy—my pale pink KitchenAid standing mixer with the adorable quilted cozy cover—and said, "Let the games begin!"

When my mom got home from work, she took one look at the chaos in the kitchen and ordered pizza; there was no way she was getting to her oven tonight.

It actually turned out to be kind of fun, baking a hundred and twenty cupcakes. My brothers were in and out, entertaining my friends, and people just ate pizza kind of casually, standing around. It felt like an event. During the small pockets of downtime, we did homework and quizzed one another for the vocab test some of us would have on Friday, and we started to feel pretty psyched that we could pull off two big cupcake orders.

Then Jake decided to help.

I heard the crash before I even realized where he was. It came from the garage, and it was loud but not that deadly kind of noise where you wonder if someone got really hurt. I ran out to the garage to find the fridge door open, Jake standing with his hands in the air, and two dozen eggs all over the garage floor.

"Jake!" I wailed, and he began to cry.

Well, I guess it wasn't the end of the world, of course, but it felt like it at first, despite my mom scolding me to lay off Jake. We ended up losing a crucial forty-five minutes while Sam (nicely) went to the store and bought more eggs. It shook us out of our rhythm and our good mood (do you know how hard it is to clean up gooey smashed eggs from concrete?), and it left us stressed and maybe not so psyched and confident about Friday. It also left us rushing through trimming many of the cupcake wrappers and making the lumps of "popcorn." Surveying our handiwork, I had to admit to myself that it was pretty amateur looking for the Cupcake Club.

By nine o'clock, everyone's parents were arriving to pick them up, and at the end of the night, I wound up on my own with everything to clean up.

The good news was that eight dozen cupcakes were arrayed on platters on the dining room table, with two dozen more cooling in the kitchen and a nice big bowl of white frosting sat in the (kitchen) fridge. Ten dozen popcorn lumps sat under foil next to a pile of ten dozen popcorn wrappers; those were the only weak links.

By the time I went to bed (again at nearly midnight), everything was in order, and I was looking forward to Friday's assembly line, if for no other reason than to get it over with. They weren't going to be the amazing professional cupcakes we liked to make, but they were something. And they were for Romaine Ford and her famous friends, after all.

Olivia brought a garment bag to school on Friday, along with a suitcase full of hair and makeup tools, jewelry and accessories, and three choices of shoes.

"Olivia, remember. This is work. You will be paid," I said, but again she waved me away.

"Emma, this could be my big break. That's where the real payday comes in. There will be tons of agents and Hollywood people there. Cupcake money looks like peanuts next to their paychecks. And, anyway, part of being successful, no matter what you do, is looking good!"

I rolled my eyes and hoped things would work out later.

After school, Olivia and the Cupcakers and I walked home to my house. I was surprised to see that Mia also had a garment bag, and even Katie and Alexis were toting small bags with outfits and supplies for the premiere.

"Guys, I just want to remind you, we are not a key part of this premiere. Romaine asked for the cupcakes kind of as a favor to, you know, include me. And there are going to be a lot of serious, real people there, working. It's Romaine's big day. Not the Cupcake Club's!"

"Oh, Emma, don't be such a stick in the mud! You never know who we'll meet along the delivery route!" Olivia laughed. I winced.

"Speaking of big days, when is Romaine getting *married*, Emma?" asked Katie. No one had asked me that point-blank since I'd found out, so I hadn't had to lie. Until now.

"Oh . . ." I searched for the right thing to say that wouldn't be a lie. "Soon. It's a secret, so . . . you know, they don't want the press to get wind of anything and ruin it. Mum's the word!" Phew. I hadn't lied.

Out of the corner of my eyes, I could feel

Olivia looking at me, and I could tell she thought I had no idea but was bluffing to make it look like I was involved. I took a deep breath. I'd have to let this one go, because I wasn't about to blow Romaine's whole cover just to make myself look good in front of Olivia Allen (no matter how tempted I was!).

Mia was thoughtful. "If I were Romaine, I'd just do it now. Like, *here*, while everyone's in town. No one would ever suspect it."

My stomach dropped. I didn't say anything.

"Are you nuts? Why would a glamorous celebrity like Romaine Ford get married in this little town when she could go anywhere on Earth?" asked Olivia, shaking her head in dismay of Mia's lack of imagination.

"I guess," said Mia, considering Olivia's point. "It depends on what kind of girl she really is."

Alexis looked at me. "Is she a hometown girl, Em, or a glamourpuss?"

"Oh, she's . . . a little bit of both," I conceded. Well, it was true! I changed the subject. "Like, I wonder what she'll wear tonight?"

"She's been wearing a lot of Ralph Lauren lately . . . ," said Mia knowledgably, and then they were off—Olivia and Mia, mainly—discussing some of the many fab outfits Romaine had recently sported.

Phew!

We reached my house, and the boys had beaten us home. Matt was there with George and his friend Charlie, and they were hungrily eyeing the cupcakes in the dining room.

"Not so fast!" I yelled. "Rejects only!" Silently, I hoped we wouldn't have as many rejects as I suspected.

I set to work getting everyone organized. Naturally, I paired Katie with George to begin piping the frosting, and of course Matt and Alexis were a team to bake tomorrow's cupcakes. I put Charlie with both Mia and Olivia (they could fight to the death to see who won him!) for the wrapping and taping of the popcorn papers; I kind of floated and tried to oversee everyone. Unfortunately, I got a little bogged down with Katie and George and the frosting, because when I went back to see how Mia and Olivia and Charlie were doing, it was not going well at all.

Olivia was mostly chatting, Charlie was all thumbs, with no standard of how to make the wrappers look good, and Mia was nearly in tears of frustration.

More than half of the cupcakes they'd wrapped looked terrible—the papers were crinkled, and some even a little ripped, like they'd been handled too roughly.

"Whoa, whoa, people! These look bad!" I exclaimed.

Charlie looked up at me in surprise. "What? I think they look great!"

Olivia was caught clearly not paying attention. "What do you mean?" she asked, only just looking down at what she was doing. With all her chatting, she'd probably only taped on three wrappers, but they weren't aligned carefully, and they looked totally lame.

"Okay. We don't have any extra wrappers to spare," I said, trying to keep the anger out of my voice. "So we need to really focus here, okay?" I looked at my watch. "We have just two hours to finish and deliver the cupcakes."

Olivia rolled her eyes a little at Charlie, and I saw her. I'd had enough. "Olivia, do you not like this job? 'Cause I can find something else for you to do, or you don't even have to do it if you don't want. You can just watch, and then we'll tell you about the premiere when we get home." I knew I was being nasty, but it worked. Olivia was not about to miss out on the event of a lifetime.

I tried another tack, then. "You know what? Charlie, maybe you should do some assembly, over by Katie and George, and let's leave the wrappers to Olivia and Mia, okay?" If I got the boy out of the picture, maybe then Olivia would concentrate.

Charlie shrugged. He didn't mind at all. It wasn't like any of the guys wanted to be *good* at making cupcakes, because that would be embarrassing. I hadn't thought of that when I signed on Matt and his friends, that it would be a badge of honor to do a bad job. Ugh. Boys are soooo weird!

Pretty soon, Mia and Olivia got into a groove and began to make progress. Olivia was so into it that her chatter died down, and she got faster and better. By the end of the process, the vast majority of the wrappers looked great, and I knew we could hide the lame ones behind the good ones on the stacked platters.

I turned back to Katie and George, the popcorn people, and got them a little back on track. They'd been chatting so much that the popcorn was sticking together and was extra lumpy, and they'd sprayed them unevenly. Boy, being a manager was hard work! I was wishing I'd had just a small focused task to do instead. I guess this is what being a movie producer feels like!

Pretty soon, I noticed everyone looking at the clock or their watches or phones. It was five fifteen, and we were due to leave for the premiere at six.

My dad arrived and complimented us on the cupcakes and said he was ready to drive at anytime. As it turned out, the boys wanted to come, too, and it would be a tight squeeze in our van, so my mom offered to drive her car too. We'd all go. A caravan. Oh goody! Not.

Finally, we packed the cupcakes—lumpy, kind of cute, definitely homemade looking—into the carriers and set them by the door. We put the final three dozen of "Mona's" cupcakes into the oven, and then it was time to run up and change. I had to let it go about these cupcakes. They were a concession—a favor—to me and, even more so, to my friends, and I had to just look at them that way. They were our humble contribution. But it just made me resolve that tomorrow's cupcakes, as simple as they were, would be our finest work.

Upstairs, Olivia and Mia took what felt like endless amounts of time getting dressed, trying different options and trading things back and forth. It was probably only ten minutes, but I was so antsy, I couldn't stand it.

When we were all ready, we scurried out with the carriers to the two vehicles and loaded in the cupcakes. Just as we were about to pull out, Olivia yelled, "Wait! There are still cupcakes in the oven!" I hopped out of the car before my dad had even totally stopped moving. Inside, I raced to the oven and pulled out the trays of cupcakes. I had caught them just in the nick of time. One more minute, and they would have been too hard and completely ruined. I set them out to cool, turned off the oven, and raced back to the minivan, where my dad reprimanded me for jumping out of a moving vehicle. Whoops.

"Olivia. You saved the day," I said, anyway, gasping.

Olivia smirked and said, "Now can we stay for the whole premiere?"

I groaned and re-buckled my seat belt.

Now underway, I was started to get jazzed. Half the cupcakes were behind us, and we were more than halfway done with the next round. Dropping them off at the premiere would be fun, and we might even get to see a star or maybe a big producer or something. Even if we didn't, it was still cool to be inside before the star of the show. How many other kids would be able to say that?

Alexis, Matt, George, and Katie were in the car with my mom, and the rest of us, plus Jake, were with my dad in the minivan. Traffic was heavy heading into town, and at the last minute, my dad decided to take a sneaky shortcut and signaled to my mom to follow. We ended up on a random, quiet country lane I don't remember ever seeing before.

"It used to be all farmland out here, not that long ago!" said my dad. "Some of these old access roads aren't really marked, and they don't turn up on the GPS, but they're still handy. Wait . . ."

There was a car pulled over up ahead of us, its hazard lights flashing. As we drew closer, I could see it was an old blue SUV.

"Wonder if these guys need help?" my dad asked, slowing down to look.

"Dad! We're going to be late! We can't stop!" I cried. But just as I said it, something about that SUV looked familiar.

It was the sticker from Sam's lacrosse team on the back window.

My dad pulled alongside and lowered down the passenger-side window in the front.

"Dad!" I yelled. "It's—"

CHAPTER 9

Clipboards

Romaine Ford popped her head out of the driver's-side window. "Oh, thank goodness! We've had a breakdown, and we're late...."

There was a collective gasp in our car as everyone realized who it was. Liam Carey leaned his head forward from the passenger seat of the Suburban, and as he came into view someone in my vehicle (I will kill him or her if I ever figure out who it was) shrieked.

I rolled down my window. "Romaine! It's Emma! We have the cupcakes!"

"Emma?" Romaine blinked at me in confusion.

"That's my dad driving. Do you want a ride?"

"Oh my goodness, Emma! Oh, this is so lucky. Yes, please! We'd love a ride! Let me just lock up."

I rolled up my window, and we scrambled to make room in the second row for Liam and Romaine. Everyone was speechless. I felt bad for the others in the car behind us for missing out, but I was psyched for Mia and Olivia. Romaine turned off her Suburban, locked it, and came around the car. Seconds later, Liam jumped into the front next to my dad and shook his hand, and Romaine clambered into the second row with Olivia and me. Olivia's eyes were wide, and her jaw had dropped in shock. Romaine gave me a hard, grateful hug and said, "Hi, guys!"

Liam turned around from the front seat and gave us all a megawatt grin and a wave. "Hi! I'm Liam!"

Like, duh!

"To the premiere!" cried my dad. "The public awaits!" And he took off.

OMG, why does my dad have to be so embarrassing?

As we drove, Romaine explained that she'd driven because the car was old and glitchy, and she wanted to take back roads to avoid the traffic and crowds on the other end. And then the engine flooded or something, and they got stuck.

"Why didn't you just get a limo, if you don't mind my asking?" my dad inquired. Embarrassing again. Like, do we have to acknowledge out loud that they're stars? Anyway, do they even have limos in Maple Grove? Come on!

"That's what I said. Maybe not a limo but someone to drive, but Romaine feels like it's her hometown, and she should be able to drive herself to the movies if she wants, right, honey?" Liam teased.

She rolled her eyes at us, but smiled. "Right. Seemed like a good idea at the time."

"We just get so harassed when we're out in LA that we like to be normal when we're here, you know?" Liam was saying to my dad.

"It's gotta be tough for you kids," my dad agreed.

"Kids"? Seriously?

Meanwhile, Olivia had not stopped staring at Romaine the entire time. It was like Romaine was a movie and Olivia was watching her.

"Um . . . hi!" Romaine said with a giggle, waving at Olivia. Olivia looked shocked out of her daydream.

I jumped in. "Oh, Romaine, this is Olivia. And you've met Mia before, at your shower, when we dropped off the cupcakes, and—"

"I'm Jake!" said Jake, popping up out from the backseat.

"Hi, Jake!" said Romaine. "You're as cute as a button!"

Jake fake-scowled, but I could tell he was pleased.

"Liam, Emma's the girl who bakes the cupcakes!" said Romaine.

"Oh, right! Thanks! They're delicious!" said Liam. "I had some after the bridal shower, when they let me back into the house. I can't wait for—"

"Yes, for *tonight*. When we have some at the *premiere*, right?" Romaine interrupted with a very significant tone of voice. I knew what she was getting at, but she masked it pretty well. Liam caught her drift too.

"Right," he said, nodding. "That's going to be the first thing I eat tonight!"

I've seen Liam Carey's abs in the movies before, and I had to doubt if he was eating very many cupcakes, but I was still psyched about the compliment.

Soon we reached the back entrance of the mall. The Press was lined up three-people deep, and onlookers were held back by a red velvet rope. There were beefy guards at the sides of the gate to the parking lot, and a lady with a clipboard and a headset, standing in front. Romaine and Liam ducked down out of sight, and I felt bad for them. They were like fugitives.

"Sorry, closed for a private event," said the lady to my dad.

"I know," said my dad. "I'm delivering cupcakes for the event."

"Name?" Clipboard Lady said.

"The Cupcake Club," my dad replied. To his credit, he wasn't even a little embarrassed saying it.

The lady scanned her list. "Sorry. Not here. Back it up." She gestured to the guards, and they stepped in to block the way.

"Wait!" I said. "We have a delivery. We're meeting . . . ?" I nudged Romaine, and she mumbled something.

Clipboard Lady sighed an exasperated sigh. "We haven't got all night. Please. Back the vehicle out."

Romaine peeped up her head a tiny bit to me and said, "Annika Dolan."

"Annika Dolan!" I called. My dad relayed the name, and Clipboard Lady said something into her headset. Then she shook her head.

"Ms. Dolan is not aware what this is in reference to. So now if you'll please turn the vehicle around, we've got cars backing up. . . ." Now Clipboard Lady was tapping her foot angrily. Even if she was using words like "please," icicles were dripping from them.

105

I felt breathless. I didn't know what to do next!

There was a long pause, and then Liam and Romaine both sat up at the same time. There was a gasp from the nearby crowd, and Clipboard Lady's eyes widened as she saw them.

"Oh . . . I *am* sorry! Please! Go right ahead!" The gate lifted, and we sailed through, my mom following close behind and the press only realizing they'd been tricked at the very last minute, when it was too late. They roared in frustration, and the sound sent chills down my spine. I watched through the back windshield as they pressed at the gate, and the guards had to physically hold them back.

But we were in! We all hooted and hollered and high-fived in relief as we entered the parking structure. My dad said he'd take us all the way to the theater level and drop us off, then wait for us outside down the street a bit.

"Okay, even if I didn't get to drive myself, that was pretty successful!" declared Romaine, laughing and clapping her hands. We all climbed out at the theater level, and the rest of the kids from the car behind us mobbed Liam and Romaine as I introduced everyone.

"Well, I've got to get this lovely lady off to her

preshow interviews," said Liam. "It was great meeting all of you. See you"—Romaine elbowed him and he laughed—"very soon!" I was glad Liam had as hard a time as I did keeping a secret!

Romaine rolled her eyes, hugged my dad, and took off. "Thanks for the cupcakes!" she called over her shoulder. "I'll tell Annika you're coming, and she'll pay you!"

After they were gone, it felt like a collective letdown, like the energy had been sucked out of a room. We unloaded the cupcake boxes, waved good-bye to my parents for the time being, and headed in.

Inside were tons of cameras and photographers, and their flashes blinded us as we entered.

"They think we're someone!" cried Olivia.

"We are!" said Alexis, laughing. "We're the Cupcake Club!" She did a little twirl, holding out the cupcake carrier, and then curtsied.

We all laughed and went to find Annika.

As we roamed the floor, I spied a big buffet, and we went to deposit the carriers there.

"Wow," said Katie, impressed. There were big glass jars of colorful—beautiful—candy and platters of incredible-looking treats. Very professional. The Cupcakers and I exchanged looks, and we all knew what we were thinking: We were definitely amateurs. There was no way *Celebrity* magazine was going to write about the Cupcake Club. Not for our contribution tonight!

Surveying the competition, Alexis looked devastated, and Katie's mouth had dropped open as she examined the treats from the other bakeries. There were triple-decker caramel fudge cupcakes with steps made from caramels climbing the sides, and tiny elaborate pastries with beautiful white cream piped into swirls on top. There were small dishes—artistic-looking crème brûlées with shellacked surfaces so shiny, I could almost see my reflection, and chocolate-dipped strawberries with long, elegant stems.

"Katie, what's that expression your mom uses when something comes out looking junky?" I asked.

Katie looked at me, nodding but looking crestfallen. "'Loving hands at home.'" She sighed as she quoted.

I had to laugh. "Yup. That's us all right. We had good intentions and lots of love, but not a whole lot of skill on display here tonight."

Mia laughed. "At least *we* look good!"

"We look great, you mean!" corrected Olivia.

Suddenly, an executive-looking lady in high, high heels and another headset came tapping over to us. "I'm Annika Dolan," she said crisply. She put out her hand, and I jumped in to shake it.

"Emma Taylor. We have the cupcakes."

"And the bill," said Alexis professionally. She handed Annika an envelope. I hadn't even thought of a bill! I smiled at Alexis and nodded in gratitude.

"Thank you," said Annika, stashing the bill into the file folder she was carrying. "Romaine asked me to help you set up, then she'd like me to direct you to your seats."

"Wait . . ." I was confused. "We're not . . . I mean . . ."

But Mia shushed me. "Thank you. It won't take a minute," said Mia.

"All right. I'll be back to collect you in five minutes. No. Make that seven," said Annika, looking at her watch. "Put them right . . . there." She gestured to a spot in the very back of the buffet, off to the side, and click-clicked away on her high heels. We all stared at one another in shock. Then the girls started to jump up and down and quietly scream and the boys did a kind of mellow high-five, as if to say, *This is cool, but it's not that big a deal.* I knew, though, that inside they were beyond psyched.

"But, guys, what about Mona's cupcakes?" I asked.

Everyone froze.

"Anyone free tomorrow at six a.m.?"

There was a brief silence, and Olivia said, "I am."

"Me too," said Matt.

"We're all free," said Alexis generously.

"Thanks, guys. Matt, will you call Mom and Dad, please, and tell them this will take a *tiny* bit longer than we thought?" I asked.

We wedged the popcorn cupcakes onto their platters in the back of the table, and then we had to giggle.

"At least we know they taste good," Katie said philosophically.

"Just don't give out our name to anyone!" said Alexis. We all had to laugh that Alexis the publicity hound wanted to remain anonymous!

One Sweet Summer was wonderful. A real romantic comedy; even the boys laughed. We didn't meet any more stars or talk to anyone famous, though. We were up in the balcony, way back in the row, with lots of other non-famous people and the press, but just being there was incredible.

Alexis was hanging so far over the railing at one

point, looking for Trent Channing, I had to yell at her. She was indignant until I gestured at Matt, like she was forgetting about him, and then she calmed down. Finally, she spotted Trent Channing and dismissed him as "short in real life," and I saw relief wash over Matt's face, as if he'd really ever been in competition with Trent Channing.

At the end of the film, everyone gave it a standing ovation. I saw Mrs. Ford and a handsome older man, who could only have been Romaine's father, down below. Romaine and Liam were kissing, and there were flashbulbs popping, and Romaine graciously waved and took a bow to acknowledge the applause. It was kind of funny to see her working live like that. As if the Romaine I know and the Romaine that belongs to the public were two different people.

It must be weird to be famous.

We left the theater and called my parents to say we were ready to leave. It was nine o'clock by this point.

Alexis was yawning and said, "Are you sure Mona needs these things by eight thirty? She doesn't even open until ten!"

"I'm sure," I said firmly. "Don't back out on me now, Cupcakers!"

"We won't," said Katie sweetly.

"Anyway, they're for Mona. They don't have to be perfect perfect," said Alexis.

I whipped my head to glare at her, but then I saw that she was smiling.

"Kidding!" she sing-songed, her palms up in the air.

"Very funny," I said. "Not."

Mia said, "Thanks so much for getting us this job, Emma. It was great."

"And thanks for including me," said Olivia. And then she smiled at me. A sweet, sincere smile. She had relaxed during the movie, and I was able to see that side of her I occasionally glimpse when she's not being competitive or nervous but is, I guess, acting like her true self.

Everyone agreed it had been awesome, even George and Charlie. Then Matt gave me the best news I'd heard all day.

"You know what, kiddo? You can keep your room," he said. "Tonight was payback enough."

I grinned. "Thanks. I'll tell Romaine I owe her one."

CHAPTER 10

Wedding Bells

$\mathcal{M}$y alarm went off at 5:45, and I was not psyched, to say the least.

I put on in a simple pink dress and went to wake up Matt. We crept down to the kitchen, where we ate some cereal and I put on an apron to protect my outfit. Olivia, Mia, and Katie rolled in soon after, and then Alexis. Six of us could definitely get this done in two hours. Everyone wondered why I had a dress on, but I explained that I'd have to stay to help Mona when we delivered the cupcakes, and I was worried I wouldn't have time to change later.

I closed the kitchen doors to keep down the noise, and we got to work. First we made a huge batch of buttercream frosting, which we divided up among five different bowls. Katie took charge of the food coloring—you needed a light hand, because pastels can quickly turn to deep colors if you're not careful—and Mia took the lead with the flavorings. The final list had arrived in my in-box yesterday: lemon, lime, rose, pear, and lavender, two dozen of each. Good thing we'd bought so many flavors in advance.

"We only want the *slightest* hint of flavor," I instructed.

"Maybe you should do it, since you're so stressed about it?" suggested Mia.

I had to admit she had a point. Carefully, I squeezed one tiny drop at a time into each of the small bowls of white frosting, then I passed them along to Katie to tint.

All the bakers were working steadily, but there wasn't the sense of urgency we'd had last night. I watched as the hands crept around the dial of the kitchen clock, and people were chatting or taking a break.

Finally, I exploded. "Guys! We need to leave here in half an hour to get the cupcakes to Mona on time! This is no joke!" I cried.

"Okay, chill. Seriously, Em," chided Matt. He gave me a look, like I was a major loser for freaking out, and shook his head.

If these people only knew, I thought.

At eight o'clock we were working on the final batch—the lavender-flavored cupcakes—when the phone rang.

It startled me so much that I accidentally dumped a big glop of flavoring into the frosting bowl.

"Nuts!" I yelled. "Matt, can you get the phone, please?"

"We can fix this. Here. Wait," said Katie calmly. She took a spoon and did a wide scoop around the small puddle of extract, then she flicked it off the spoon and into the trash. "Give it a stir. I bet it's okay."

"Phone's for you, Em," said Matt. "It's Mona."

I quickly tasted the frosting, and it was fine. I went to pick up the phone.

"Hello, Mona?" I said.

"Hello, darling. Listen. Patricia and I will come to you at eight thirty, all righty? We'd like to get a bit of a hop, and we're just sitting here. See you soon?"

I gulped. Only about a fifth of the cakes were frosted, and we had about twenty-five minutes left. "Okay. See you soon!" I said, and hung up.

I watched as Katie took the final bowl—the

lavender-flavored frosting—and dropped in two tiny dark drops of color. She began to stir, and to my shock, the frosting began to turn pale green as the color mixed in.

"Katie!" I yelled.

"What?" she jumped, nearly dropping the food coloring into the bowl. Then she recovered and put the jar aside.

"That's the lavender-flavored frosting!" I cried.

"No, it's not! Lavender is over there!" She gestured across the island, and sure enough, there was a bowl of very pale purple frosting.

I surveyed the other colors. "Then which one is lime?"

"Oh no." Katie groaned.

Quickly, we began tasting the flavors with toothpicks, comparing the flavors with the frostings' colors.

"Okay, the pink one . . . that's lime," said Mia. "For sure."

"The green is lemon. Definitely," said Alexis.

I put my head in my hands.

"Oh, Emma, I'm so sorry!" Katie wailed.

My mouth set into a grim line. "Well, it is what it is. Now we just have to make them look perfect."

Everyone lined up, and in a very efficient

manner, we quickly frosted all the cupcakes, each with a beautifully piped swirl of pastel frosting on top. Mia and Katie did most of it, and they looked perfect—simple but elegant. We arranged them into the carriers (newly vacated by the popcorn cupcakes), and as I set the last carrier down by the door, Mona pulled up in in her van.

My mom came down and reviewed the stacks of cupcakes. "Oh, girls, these are lovely! So sweet and simple. But absolutely beautiful."

Matt cleared his throat. "Ahem. 'Girls'?" He pretended to look indignant.

"Sorry, lovebug," said my mom, patting his cheek. "These are some of the prettiest cupcakes you've ever made. Like little works of art."

Matt pretended to duck his head in modesty. "Thank you," he said, wiping away a fake tear.

"All right, Mr. Academy Award winner, why don't you help us get these into the van?" I said.

"Oh, I forgot the bill!" said Alexis.

"That's what you get for staying out late and hobnobbing with the stars all night," teased Mia.

"I have something. I can e-mail it over later," I said. Again, I didn't lie. I just didn't say who I'd be e-mailing it to!

We trucked all the carriers outside, and Mona

and Patricia hopped out of the van. I yanked off my apron.

"Hey, Emma, just a quick thought," said Mona, gesturing me to the side of the van.

Oh no. Had she seen the cupcakes and thought they were lame? Inside, I was dying of shame. We should have made a bigger effort. We should have gone all out. I knew it. But no, Mona was saying something else.

". . . a little more help?"

"What?" I asked. I was confused.

"Do you think your friends would like to come? They could set up the cupcakes and help me get the ladies ready?"

My eyes widened. "Do I! Of course! Do you want to ask them or should I?"

Mona smiled. "I will." She went back toward the house, clapping her hands. "Girls! Girls! I need a little help. Does anyone have time to come with me this morning?"

Katie and Mia eagerly volunteered. Alexis noted that she had a lot of homework, and Olivia was very hesitant.

"Come on, you guys. We need to get going. Just say yes. It will be fun, and it won't take long," I said. My eyes must've been shining, because they were all looking at me suspiciously.

"Let me just run in and call my mom," said Olivia. The others joined her and scrambled back outside. Olivia had brushed her hair and even put on a little clear lip gloss.

"You look pretty," I said, before I even realized what was coming out of my mouth.

"Thanks," said Olivia shyly. "You never know where your next job is going to come from, right?" She'd been called in to model at The Special Day before, so she probably figured there might be business at hand. Little did she know.

"All aboard!" Mona called, and everyone climbed in. So all the Cupcake girls were aboard plus one, Olivia. Matt decided to sit this one out.

We set off, and people began asking questions.

"Wait, we're not going to the store?" asked Alexis, noticing our route.

"Is this an off-site thing?" asked Mia.

The girls exchanged glances. Mona and I made eye contact in the rearview mirror and smiled at each other.

Soon, we reached the white gate at the bottom of the Fords' driveway. There was a guy sitting outside in a white chair with a clipboard, and Mona spoke to him through her window.

"Delivery from The Special Day bridal salon!"

He smiled and nodded and opened the gate, and up we rolled.

"Wait, isn't this ...?" Olivia looked around, suddenly alert.

"This is Romaine Ford's house!" cried Katie.

"We're delivering Romaine Ford's wedding dress to her house!" Mia yelled.

"To her wedding," I said.

A hush fell over the van as everyone began to understand what was going on.

"Wait, you mean those cupcakes ...," said Alexis.

"Are Romaine Ford's *wedding* cupcakes?" Olivia shrieked. (Aha! So *she* was the one who'd shrieked in the car last night!)

Mona and I laughed as she put the van into park in the back of the driveway.

"Yup," I said.

"OMG. OMG. OMG!" Katie was bouncing up and down in her seat.

"When did you find out?" asked Alexis.

"About a week ago?" I said.

"But how did you keep it a secret?" Katie demanded.

"Not very easily," I admitted. "It was soooo hard."

"I can't believe you didn't breathe a word," Mia said admiringly.

Then Alexis said, "Emma, you should have told us! We could have come up with something spectacular! Something special! These are just standard cupcakes!"

"And we don't have a special presentation!" wailed Mia.

Suddenly, I felt terrible. Maybe I had handled this wrong. After all, who was my loyalty really to—some random celebrity I barely know or my closest and best friends (and business partners)? Now they felt like yet again they were not putting forward their best work, and it was all my fault.

But then Katie jumped in. "You know what? I think these cupcakes are perfect. Look around. Romaine is getting married in her backyard. It isn't fancy. And these cupcakes are really pretty; even your mom kept saying so. I think they are just perfect."

I let out my breath, and suddenly, I felt Mona's arm across my shoulders.

"I agree," said Mona. "Simple elegance always is the chicest. Trust me. And I think the bride will agree too."

And just then Romaine came out onto the

porch. She did not look like last night's glamorous movie premiere star, in fancy makeup with a fancy hairdo and gown. She looked like . . . well, like the girl next door! Fresh-scrubbed face, wet hair, sweats, and a huge, happy smile on her face.

"Hi, Emma!" she says. "Hi, Cupcakers!"

The girls were all speechless and Romaine laughed. "Surprise! Now let's see the cupcakes. I've been waiting all week!"

We climbed the porch stairs, and Romaine sat on one of the wicker settees as I opened the lid of one of the carrying cases.

"OH!" cried Romaine. "They're absolutely perfect. It's just what I wanted!" Then she got a devilish look in her eye. "Can I taste one?"

"Of course!" I said. "They're your cupcakes!"

Romaine bit into one, and her eyes got big. "These are delicious!" she said through a mouthful of crumbs. She eyed the purple frosting, and then she said, "Lime, I think?"

"Yeah, um, about the flavors? They don't exactly match the colors. . . . I'm so sorry."

"It's all my fault." Katie began to apologize profusely.

"I think it's genius!" said Romaine. "How boring would it be if the flavors matched the colors?

122

Anyone could do that! This is unexpected; professional cupcakes with a homemade twist."

"That's us!" said Alexis proudly. Then she mumbled, "Maybe that should be our motto." We all rolled our eyes.

"All right, darlings, let's get going," says Mona, breaking the spell. She shooed Romaine into the house to get ready and asked me to follow along to help tie bows and zip up dresses after I finished setting up the cupcakes.

In the kitchen, Mrs. Ford asked the caterer to lead us out to the tent to put the cupcakes on the buffet.

There, on the dessert table, were six beautiful, pastel-colored display platters of varying heights. The caterer directed us to put the cupcakes on the pedestals, front and center, and we arranged them as instructed.

"I have an idea," Katie whispered, and she darted off into the garden.

She came back with an armful of flowers.

"Katie!" I yelped.

"Shh," she said. "I took them from the back of the garden. It's fine."

Then she and Mia began arranging the flowers around the cupcakes, peeling off the petals and delicately placing them all over the pedestals.

Once the platters were covered, we stepped back to admire our handiwork.

"Wow," said Olivia. "They really look beautiful."

They really, really did. The cupcakes were pretty, but the flowers made them perfect. It almost looked like the cupcakes were blooming out of them. I beamed, glad to know I could count on my friends.

"I can't believe it!" I said.

"Didn't you trust us?" said Alexis, hugging me with one arm.

I fake-glared at her sideways. "Not exactly. But they do look perfect."

"And I bet they taste great," said Mia.

"They match with everything in here," Katie pointed out.

We looked around, and it was true. All the tablecloths and napkins were in mix-and-match variations of the same colors, and the bouquet centerpiece on each table had flowers in the same pale yellow, green, pink, purple, and blue.

"It's all so pretty," I said.

"Funny that the cupcakes we slaved over came out sort of crummy, and the ones we just . . . did . . . came out better," Katie said.

"That's because we were trying too hard on the

other ones," admitted Mia. I was glad someone else had said it besides me.

"I just can't believe I hang out with the Cupcake Club for twenty-four hours and get to attend the two most exciting events of the year!" said Olivia. "Thanks, you guys."

"Yoo-hoo! Emma!" Patricia was calling me from the porch.

"Gotta run, guys. I'll come find you when it's time to go."

"What should we do in the meantime?" asked Katie.

"Um. I'll send Patricia down to find you, and then maybe we can all stay and spy on the wedding ceremony, okay? Just don't call the press while you're waiting. Actually, don't call anyone!"

"As if!" They all laughed.

CHAPTER 11

A Recipe for Success

𝓘'd been helping Samantha (she signed autographs for all the Cupcakers downstairs!) and Romaine's sister Florence and niece (who did look a lot like me, by the way), and when it was time for the bridal party to get together at the top of the front stairs for the procession, I saw Romaine fully dressed for the first time. I actually had tears in my eyes, she looked so beautiful.

"Oh!" I said. It was so unexpected. I mean, she's a beautiful girl, and I've seen her dressed up before. But this was different. She looked so, so happy, like she was really about to start a new life and live happily ever after. She looked like a real-life fairy princess.

I grabbed a tissue from a box on the hall table

and blotted my eyes. I felt a hand on my shoulder, and I looked up. It was Mona.

"It never gets old," she said, wiping at her own eyes. "That's why I keep doing it."

I smiled up at her. "Do you ever get sick of the brides?" I whispered.

"Oh, honey, you can't imagine!" Mona laughed. "But not this one. She's the real deal. Anyway, I like them all by the time I'm looking at the backs of them heading down the aisle. It's always a fresh start."

We trailed behind the bridal party as they made their way toward the door that led out to the garden.

"Psst!" we heard, and we turned to see Patricia waving us into the family room.

Inside were the Cupcakers and Patricia, who were awed by their privileged spot at the window. Mona and I joined them and watched as Romaine gracefully made her way through the beautiful garden, upon a white satin runner covered in rose petals, through the rows of white chairs holding only family and friends.

The look on Liam's face was breathtaking as he saw her. His eyes lit up, and he grinned till it looked like his face would break. When he took her arm, he had to accept a hankie from his best man and blot his eyes. It was so sweet. We all sighed in unison, then laughed quietly because we all had the same reaction.

"This is one of the prettiest things I've ever seen," I said.

"Me too." Mona sighed, and we giggled.

Later, on the way back to my house, with Patricia at the wheel (Mona had stayed to help with wardrobe details, and Patricia would return to help too once she'd dropped us off safely), Alexis burst out.

"I still can't believe you didn't tell us!" she chided.

"I felt terrible about it," I admitted. "And it wasn't that I didn't trust you. But if one of us slipped and it got out . . ."

"I'm glad you didn't tell us," said Katie. "It would be too much to keep that news a secret. I'm relieved!"

"I agree," said Mia. "No pressure this way!"

"You can always tell me," said Olivia. "I'm the quietest of all the Cupcake Club!" and we all laughed.

Two days later I was doing my homework when the phone rang.

"Honey, it's Alexis!" my mom called.

I sat still in my seat. Did "honey" mean me or Matt? It was really annoying to not know.

"Emma!" my mom called again.

I jumped up, pleased that the call was for me and not Matt. *Ha! So there!* I thought as I passed the room he was still sharing with Sam.

"Hello?"

"Are you on the cordless?" asked Alexis with absolutely no introduction.

"Yeeeees?" I said suspiciously.

"Go to you computer. Go to celebritymag.com. Go!"

"Okay, okay!" I scurried into my room and did as I was told. On the homepage was a story about "Romaine and Liam's Wild Weekend!" I rolled my eyes. I would hardly have called that weekend wild, but whatever.

"Click on the Romaine story," instructed Alexis, so I did. "Scroll to the end of the story. Read the second to last paragraph." I could practically hear Alexis tapping her foot impatiently while I got to the right spot and read.

"OMG!" I yelled. "I can't believe it!"

Alexis was screaming through the phone. What it said was:

Desserts for both events were catered by the Cupcake Club, a local company run by old family friends of the Fords'. The bridal cupcake display was spectacular, with an elegant array of pastel-colored cupcakes sprinkled with spring blooms matching the decor. "They make the most delicious cupcakes you've ever had," said Romaine. "Their motto is: Professional cupcakes with a homemade twist." The same could be said about Ms. Ford.

I shrieked. "This is amazing! Better publicity than we could ever dream of! Are you ecstatic?" I cried.

"Our website has already crashed twice!" said Alexis. "It's great!"

We laughed and laughed. "We need a cupcake meeting tomorrow to celebrate, don't you think?"

"Definitely," agreed Alexis.

❁

The next day we sat around Alexis's neat kitchen, discussing the Romaine Weekend, as we'd come to call it, for the tenth time.

"Pretty surprising Olivia turned out to be so handy," Mia remarked.

"Yeah, she's pretty good with her hands," I said.

"And she's got a decent work ethic, too, once you know what motivates her," agreed Alexis.

"Time for a fifth cupcake member?" asked Katie.

"Nah. Not yet," I said. "But we do need to make a note to share some of the profits with her."

Mona had dropped off a check from the Fords for the cupcakes, and Alexis was depositing it, along with the one from Romaine for the premiere cupcakes, tomorrow.

We scrolled through the pictures we'd taken at the premiere and at the wedding with our phones. We had promised Mrs. Ford we'd never e-mail them or send them anywhere, especially to be published.

"I know I can count on you girls," she e-mailed. "I can't wait until we have something else to celebrate, so we can hire you again!"

We had all cheered when we read that.

I brought a tray of the "reject" cupcakes—they still tasted delicious, but didn't look as pretty as the others (I'm guessing they were the ones Matt frosted), so they didn't make the final cut. Alexis put out a jug of milk and some glasses on the table.

"What next?" asked Mia.

"Isabel Gormley's birthday!" said Alexis, looking at a list.

"Oh, the cupcake competition with the kits!"

"That's going to be so cool!" said Katie.

"And so easy," added Mia, "compared to a movie premiere."

"Not so fast!" I cautioned, wagging my finger at her.

She laughed and put her hands in the air like *I surrender.*

Alexis picked up where I'd left off. "Remember, our best clients, like the Gormleys—and Mona—are the most important ones to please. And our simplest cupcakes are the ones we need to work on the hardest. It's all the opposite of what you'd think."

"A recipe for success if ever there was one," I said admiringly. I held up a cupcake for a toast. "To Romaine and Liam."

"And to the Cupcake Club!" Mia added. We all clinked cupcakes together and laughed. It was the perfect end to a perfect (not wild!) weekend.

Want another sweet cupcake?

Here's a sneak peek
of the twentieth book in the

CUPCAKE DIARIES

series:

Alexis
the icing on the
cupcake

Growth Spurt

$\mathcal{M}$y ankles were freezing.

It was a cold and rainy morning, even though it was almost Memorial Day, and the weather was a little fluky: hot and muggy one day, chilly and cool the next. So maybe that explained my cold ankles. But the rest of me wasn't chilly. My ankles felt . . . bare, despite the fact I had on long pants. I stretched out my foot at the breakfast table and looked down. Wait, why was there suddenly so much ankle showing from the bottom of my pant leg? These pants weren't capris! Had they shrunk?

I stood up and shimmied the pants down a little so that they covered more of my ankles. My older sister, Dylan, gave me glance over her teapot and then looked back at what she was reading. Now my ankles were covered, but my pants were riding too low for comfort. They were practically falling off my hips, actually.

"Argh!" I cried in frustration.

"What's the matter, Lex?" asked Dylan in a slightly annoyed tone. "I'm trying to have a peaceful morning here." Dylan's been trying to be all mature these days, drinking tea and acting really patient and calm no matter what the situation. She took this relaxation and meditation class, and now she goes around telling us that the house has to be her "Zen place."

"My pants don't fit!" I cried very un-Zenlike. "And they're not that old! I just bought them with Grandma over spring break!"

Dylan rolled her eyes. "You must've shrunk them. You're supposed to line dry cotton pants like that."

"I do!" I protested. "Always!"

Dylan thought for a minute, then she sighed and shook her head. "Then it could only be one thing," she said, returning to the fascinating back of the cereal box.

I guess she wasn't going to tell me unless I asked. And I really, *really* didn't want to ask. But the suspense was killing me.

"What?"

Dylan sighed again, as if it was all so obvious and I was such a nitwit. "Hello? Growth spurt!"

"What?"

"You grew! Happens all the time. That's why they call it 'growing up.'" She shook her head.

"But that *fast*?"

She nodded. "It can happen overnight sometimes. You come down in the morning and suddenly you can see things on the top shelf of the fridge that you'd swear you couldn't see when you went to bed the night before."

"Really?" I walked over to the fridge and opened it. I glanced around the top shelf: yogurt, pickles, mustard . . . Wait, had that temperature dial always been back there? I knew I'd never seen it before because I would have had some fun tweaking it to see if different temperatures saved us money or made things icy. Had the fridge really come like that? I didn't dare ask Dylan.

Feeling slightly freaked out, I shut the door and stood with my back to it, hands still on the handle.

There was no doubt about it.

I had grown.

"So what should I do?" I asked Dylan.

"About what?"

I gestured helplessly at my naked ankles.

Dylan stood up to wash her cup in the sink. "Buy new pants," she said.

Before I could go to school, I had to change my pants, but I had to try on two other pairs before I found one that fit. At school I ran into my best friend, Emma Taylor, on the way to my locker.

"I grew," I said, falling into step beside her.

"I know," she agreed.

I stopped dead in my tracks. "Wait! *Really?* You could tell?"

Emma stopped too and nodded. "Uh-huh. I have to look up at you when I talk to you now."

"Well, when were you going to tell me?"

Emma laughed and started walking again. "Seriously, Lexi? You need me to *tell* you that you grew?"

"I don't know. I mean, it's not like I noticed it myself." I unlocked my locker and was startled to see how packed my top shelf was. "Ugh. This locker is a pit. I need to clean this thing out!"

Emma laughed again. "See? Suddenly, you can see stuff that's high up. Maybe you could check the top shelf in my locker and see if my mouth guard for soccer is up there."

I laughed. "What, now I'm renting out my height?"

She giggled. "You could!"

"What, for locker cleanouts?"

"Yeah, you could charge. . . ."

My money-making senses tingled a little. I do have a head for business. Could I earn cash by cleaning out lockers? Probably. The bigger question is, would I want to? A thought for another day.

Speaking of money . . . "Hey, are we meeting today?" I asked. Our Cupcake Club usually meets on Fridays at lunch to plan out upcoming jobs and experiment with new recipes, as well as bake for our regular customers and any weekend jobs we might have lined up. Plus, we always get together at Friday lunch and bring cupcakes; it's a delicious tradition.

"Yup," said Emma. "We have our lunch meeting, obviously, and then after school we're on for baking. Mia can come now that she'll be at her mom's this weekend. Let's do it at my house."

"Great. I brought the ledger and everything, just in case we were able to meet. I'll see you later in the cafeteria," I said, and we headed off to our classes.

Down the hall, I stopped for a quick gulp of

water at the fountain. I swear, I've never noticed how low that thing is. It's, like, elementary school–size! They should really have it raised.

"Lexxxiiiiii!" called Mia from our table in the corner. I cringed a little and glanced around to see if anyone else had heard her call me that. It's not that I really mind if my family or my very closest friends call me "Lexi" in private, it's just that lately it has been rubbing me the wrong way. It sounds babyish, and I don't want it to spread. And also, just secretly, it does bug me a teeny, tiny bit when Mia and Katie call me "Lexi" because it's really my childhood nickname from before I knew them. Like, they don't really have the right to call me that. But whatever.

I crossed the lunchroom with my tray and went to sit beside Mia.

"What's up?" asked Mia. "Cute pants. Haven't seen those before."

Mia is a major fashionista (her mom is a professional stylist), so I always pay close attention to her fashion advice.

"Seriously? Do you like these pants?" I asked, looking down. "I've had them for a while, but they were always too big. Now they fit. They cover my ankles, anyway." I shrugged.

"Definitely cute. My faves are your pale pink ones, though."

I sighed and picked up a forkful of chili. "They shrank. Or, actually, I grew. They don't fit anymore already!"

"Can't you get them shortened a little more and wear them as capris?" she asked. "They'd be cute with a white sleeveless blouse."

I chewed my chili and thought about it. "Maybe. The thing is . . . I don't look so good in cropped pants."

"Oh, come on! With those long, thin legs of yours, you'd look good in anything," said Mia.

I couldn't help but smile a little, since a compliment from Mia means a lot. "Thanks. I'm not sure that's true, but whatever."

"Oh please, I'd kill to be tall and thin like you." At that point in the conversation, Emma and Katie joined us. I did feel a little better after what Mia said about my figure, even though I was still frustrated about my wardrobe.

"Hey, listen, we got a good order over the weekend," said Katie. "Remember Mrs. Dreher who had the baby shower? She's having a summer kick-off barbecue slash pool party next Sunday, and she wants us to bake six dozen 'beachy' cupcakes."

"Great!" I said. "Did you quote her a price or should I follow up?"

Katie smiled. "I gave her a ballpark price and said our CFO would follow up with an e-mail once we knew for sure what we were baking."

"Excellent." I nodded happily. I love it when our business runs like a well-oiled machine.

Mia started brainstorming. "Remember those cool pool cupcakes we did for the swim team fundraiser? Maybe we should do those again?"

"Oh, but remember how the frosting melted on those when it got hot in the indoor pool area?" reminded Emma. "We wouldn't want that to happen if it's a hot day for the barbecue."

I groaned at the memory. That swim team episode had almost been a major catastrophe. We'd almost ended up *losing* money, which is something I hate!

"Let's do something with light brown sugar around the edges—like fake sand?" suggested Katie.

"Ooh, that's good!" agreed Mia.

Emma's eyes sparkled suddenly. "I think we need a field trip!" she said. "Let's go to the beach!"

"Yes!" exclaimed Mia. "When?"

Emma shrugged and looked around at all of us. "This weekend?"

I thought about my schedule. We have exams next week, and I have a big paper due. Of course, I've been studying, so I'm in pretty good shape for the tests. And I'm more than halfway done with the paper. Plus, I have the rest of it mapped out. I knew Mom and Dad would be okay with the plan. "I'm up for it!" I said.

Everyone agreed. We'd go tomorrow, providing all the parents said it was okay, and we'd still have Sunday for homework.

"Yay!" said Katie, clapping her hands. "I can wear my new swimsuit!"

Hmm. Mentally, I scanned my closet to think about what I'd wear. I guess I wouldn't know until I went home and tried things on. I was not looking forward to it.

All About Emma!

How well do you know Emma Taylor?
Take this quiz and find out!

(If you don't want to write in your book,
use a separate piece of paper.)

1. Emma is
   A. a tomboy.
   B. a girly girl.
   C. a baseball champ.
   D. a science whiz.

2. Emma has a crush on
   A. George.
   B. Dan.
   C. Diego.
   D. Joe.

3. Besides baking cupcakes, Emma works as
   A. a dog walker.
   B. a model.
   C. a fashion designer.
   D. both A and B.

4. Alexis has a crush on one of Emma's brothers. Which one?

 A. Jake

 B. Matt

 C. Sam

 D. Frank

5. What is Emma's favorite color?

 A. Purple

 B. Pink

 C. Turqoise

 D. She doesn't have a favorite color.

6. Emma loves all the Cupcake girls, but who is her BFF?

 A. Mia

 B. Alexis

 C. Katie

 D. Olivia

7. What is Emma afraid of?
    A. Spiders
    B. Mice
    C. Blood
    D. Snakes

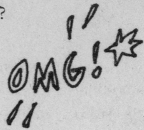

6. What movie star considers Emma her friend?
    A. Angelina Jolie
    B. Sandra Bullock
    C. Kate Winslet
    D. Romaine Ford

☆ ☆ Did you get the right answers? ☆ ☆

1. B   2. C   3. D   4. B   5. B   6. B   7. C   8. D

How did you do?

All 8 correct: You're Emma's new BFF! Three cupcakes for you. Yay!

6-7 correct: You did very well. Emma is sure you'll get all the answers right next time. Two cupcakes for you!

4-5 correct: Emma thinks you need to learn a little more about her. But you get a cupcake for trying!

Fewer than 4 correct: Emma says you're not paying attention! You need to reread the Emma stories right now! No cupcake for you until you do—but Emma says you can have a cookie. ☺

Coco Simon always dreamed of opening a cupcake bakery but was afraid she would eat all of the profits. When she's not daydreaming about cupcakes, Coco edits children's books and has written close to one hundred books for children, tweens, and young adults, which is a lot less than the number of cupcakes she's eaten. Cupcake Diaries is the first time Coco has mixed her love of cupcakes with writing.

Want more

CUPCAKEDIARIES?

Visit **CupcakeDiariesBooks.com**
for the series trailer, excerpts, activities,
and everything you need for throwing
your own cupcake party!

Still Hungry?
There's always room for another Cupcake!

Katie and the Cupcake Cure
1

Mia in the Mix
2

Emma on Thin Icing
3

Alexis and the Perfect Recipe
4

Katie, Batter Up!
5

Mia's Baker's Dozen
6

Emma All Stirred Up!
7

Alexis Cool as a Cupcake
8

Katie and the Cupcake War
9

Looking for another great book?
Find it in the middle.

in
the
middle

BOOKS

Fun, fantastic books for kids
in the in-beTWEEN age.

IntheMiddleBooks.com

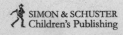

If you liked

CUPCaKe 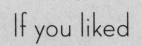 DIARIES

be sure to check out these

other series from

Simon Spotlight